International Acclaim for *Bernhard Schlink*'s

THE

$\mathcal{R}$EADER WITHDRAWN

"Arresting, philosophically elegant, morally complex.
. . . Mr. Schlink tells this story with marvelous
directness and simplicity, his writing stripped bare
of any of the standard gimmicks of dramatization."
—*The New York Times*

"The best novel I read this year . . . an unforgettable
short tale about love, horror and mercy."

rson,
Year

h its
ut
ch

of
ry
."

he

de

Bernhard Schlink

THE
ℛEADER

Bernhard Schlink was born in Germany in 1944.
A professor of law at the University of Berlin and
a practicing judge, he is also the author of several
prize-winning crime novels. He lives in Bonn
and Berlin.

INTERNATIONAL

THE
$\mathcal{R}$EADER

Bernhard Schlink

TRANSLATED FROM THE GERMAN

BY CAROL BROWN JANEWAY

Vintage International

VINTAGE BOOKS

A DIVISION OF RANDOM HOUSE, INC.

NEW YORK

FIRST VINTAGE INTERNATIONAL EDITION, OCTOBER 1998

The Library of Congress has cataloged
the Pantheon edition as follows:

Schlink, Bernhard.
[Vorleser. English]
The reader / Bernhard Schlink; translated from
the German by Carol Brown Janeway.
p.   cm.
ISBN 0-679-44279-0
I. Janeway, Carol Brown. II. Title.
PT2680.L54V6713   1997
833'.914—dc21   97-1511
CIP

Vintage ISBN: 0-679-78130-7

Author photograph © Elena Seibert
Book design by Trina Stahl

Random House Web address: www.randomhouse.com

Printed in the United States of America
20 19 18 17 16 15 14 13 12 11

PART ONE

CHAPTER ONE

WHEN I was fifteen, I got hepatitis. It started in the fall and lasted until spring. As the old year darkened and turned colder, I got weaker and weaker. Things didn't start to improve until the new year. January was warm, and my mother moved my bed out onto the balcony. I saw sky, sun, clouds, and heard the voices of children playing in the courtyard. As dusk came one evening in February, there was the sound of a blackbird singing.

The first time I ventured outside, it was to go from Blumenstrasse, where we lived on the second floor of a massive turn-of-the-century building, to Bahnhofstrasse. That's where I'd thrown up on the way home from school one day the previous October. I'd been feeling weak for days, in a way that was completely new to me. Every step was an effort. When I was faced with stairs either at home or at school, my legs would hardly carry me. I had no appetite. Even if I sat down at the table hungry, I soon felt queasy. I woke up every morning with a dry mouth and the sensation that my insides were in the wrong place and too heavy for my body. I was ashamed of being so weak. I was even more ashamed when I threw up. That was another thing that had never happened to me before. My mouth was suddenly full, I tried to swallow everything down again, and clenched my teeth with my hand in front of my mouth, but it all burst out of my mouth anyway straight through my fingers. I leaned against the wall of the building, looked down at the vomit around my feet, and retched something clear and sticky.

When rescue came, it was almost an assault. The woman seized my arm and pulled me through the dark entryway into the courtyard. Up above there were lines strung from window to window, loaded with laundry. Wood was stacked in the courtyard; in an open workshop a saw screamed and shavings flew. The woman turned on the tap, washed my hand first, and then cupped both of hers and threw water in my face. I dried myself with a handkerchief.

"Get that one!" There were two pails standing by the faucet; she grabbed one and filled it. I took the other one, filled it, and followed her through the entryway. She swung her arm, the water sluiced down across the walk and washed the vomit into the gutter. Then she took my pail and sent a second wave of water across the walk.

When she straightened up, she saw I was crying. "Hey, kid," she said, startled, "hey, kid"—and took me in her arms. I wasn't much taller than she was, I could feel her breasts against my chest. I smelled the sourness of my own breath and felt her fresh sweat as she held me, and didn't know where to look. I stopped crying.

She asked me where I lived, put the pails down in the entryway, and took me home, walking beside me holding my schoolbag in one hand and my arm in the other. It's no great distance from Bahnhofstrasse to Blumenstrasse. She walked quickly, and her decisiveness helped me to keep pace with her. She said goodbye in front of our building.

That same day my mother called in the doctor, who diagnosed hepatitis. At some point I told my mother about the woman. If it hadn't been for that, I don't think I would have gone to see her. But my mother simply assumed that as soon as I was better, I would use my pocket money to buy some flowers, go introduce myself, and say thank you, which was why at the end of February I found myself heading for Bahnhofstrasse.

CHAPTER TWO

HE BUILDING on Bahnhofstrasse is no longer there. I don't know when or why it was torn down. I was away from my hometown for many years. The new building, which must have been put up in the seventies or eighties, has five floors plus finished space under the roof, is devoid of balconies or arched windows, and its smooth façade is an expanse of pale plaster. A plethora of doorbells indicates a plethora of tiny apartments, with tenants moving in and out as casually as you would pick up and return a rented car. There's a computer store on the ground floor where once there were a pharmacy, a supermarket, and a video store.

The old building was as tall, but with only four floors, a first floor of faceted sandstone blocks, and above it three floors of brickwork with sandstone arches, balconies, and window surrounds. Several steps led up to the first floor and the stairwell; they were wide at the bottom, narrower above, set between walls topped with iron banisters and curving outwards at street level. The front door was flanked by pillars, and from the corners of the architrave one lion looked up Bahnhofstrasse while another looked down. The entryway through which the woman had led me to the tap in the courtyard was a side entrance.

I had been aware of this building since I was a little boy. It dominated the whole row. I used to think that if it made itself any heavier and wider, the neighboring buildings would have to move aside and make room for it. Inside, I imagined a stairwell with plaster moldings, mirrors, and an oriental runner held down with highly polished brass rods. I assumed that grand people would live in such a grand building. But because the building had darkened with the passing of the years and the smoke of the trains, I imagined that the grand inhabitants would be just as somber, and somehow peculiar—deaf or dumb or hunchbacked or lame.

In later years I dreamed about the building again and again. The dreams were similar, variations on one dream and one theme. I'm walking through a strange town and I see the house. It's one in a row of buildings in a district I don't know. I go on, confused, because the house is familiar but its surroundings are not. Then I realize that I've seen the house before. I'm not picturing Bahnhofstrasse in my hometown, but another city, or another country. For example, in my dream I'm in Rome, see the house, and realize I've seen it already in Bern. This dream recognition comforts me; seeing the house again in different surroundings is no more surprising than encountering an old friend by chance in a strange place. I turn around, walk back to the house, and climb the steps. I want to go in. I turn the door handle.

If I see the house somewhere in the country, the dream is more long-drawn-out, or I remember its details better. I'm driving a car. I see the house on the right and keep going, confused at first only by the fact that such an obviously urban building is standing there in the middle of the countryside. Then I realize that this is not the first time I've seen it, and I'm doubly confused. When I remember where I've seen it before, I turn around and drive back. In the dream, the road is always empty, as I can turn around with my tires squealing and race back. I'm afraid I'll be too late, and I drive faster. Then I see it. It is surrounded by fields, rape or wheat or vines in the Palatinate, lavender in Provence. The landscape is flat, or at most gently rolling. There are no trees. The day is cloudless, the sun is shining, the air shimmers and the road glitters in the heat. The fire walls make the building look unprepossessing and cut off. They could be the firewalls of any building. The house is no darker than it was on Bahnhofstrasse, but the windows are so dusty that you can't see anything inside the rooms, not even the curtains; it looks blind.

I stop on the side of the road and walk over to the entrance. There's nobody about, not a sound to be heard, not even a distant engine, a gust of wind, a bird. The world is dead. I go up the steps and turn the knob.

But I do not open the door. I wake up knowing simply that I took hold of the knob and turned it. Then the whole dream comes back to me, and I know that I've dreamed it before.

CHAPTER THREE

I DIDN'T KNOW the woman's name. Clutching my bunch of flowers, I hesitated in front of the door and all the bells. I would rather have turned around and left, but then a man came out of the building, asked who I was looking for, and directed me to Frau Schmitz on the third floor.

No decorative plaster, no mirrors, no runner. Whatever unpretentious beauty the stairwell might once have had, it could never have been comparable to the grandeur of the façade, and it was long gone in any case. The red paint on the stairs had worn through in the middle, the stamped green linoleum that was glued on the walls to shoulder height was rubbed away to nothing, and bits of string had been stretched across the gaps in the banisters. It smelled of cleaning fluid. Perhaps I only became aware of all this some time later. It was always just as shabby and just as clean, and there was always the same smell of cleaning fluid, sometimes mixed with the smell of cabbage or beans, or fried food or boiling laundry.

I never learned a thing about the other people who lived in the building apart from these smells, the mats outside the apartment doors, and the name-plates under the doorbells. I cannot even remember meeting another tenant on the stairs.

Nor do I remember how I greeted Frau Schmitz. I had probably prepared two or three sentences about my illness and her help and how grateful I was, and recited them to her. She led me into the kitchen.

It was the largest room in the apartment, and contained a stove and sink, a tub and a boiler, a table, two chairs, a kitchen cabinet, a wardrobe, and a couch with a red velvet spread thrown over it. There was no window. Light came in through the panes of the door leading out onto the balcony—not much light; the kitchen was only bright when the door was open. Then you heard the scream of the saws from the carpenter's shop in the yard and smelled the smell of wood.

The apartment also had a small, cramped living room with a dresser, a table, four chairs, a wing chair, and a coal stove. It was almost never heated in winter, nor was it used much in summer either. The window faced Bahnhofstrasse, with a view of what had been the railroad station, but was now being excavated and already in places held the freshly laid foundations of the new courthouse and administration buildings. Finally, the apartment also had a windowless toilet. When the toilet smelled, so did the hall.

I don't remember what we talked about in the kitchen. Frau Schmitz was ironing; she had spread a woolen blanket and a linen cloth over the table; lifting one piece of laundry after another from the basket, she ironed them, folded them, and laid them on one of the two chairs. I sat on the other. She also ironed her underwear, and I didn't want to look, but I couldn't help looking. She was wearing a sleeveless smock, blue with little pale red flowers on it. Her shoulder-length, ash-blond hair was fastened with a clip at the back of her neck. Her bare arms were pale. Her gestures of lifting the iron, using it, setting it down again, and then folding and putting away the laundry were an exercise in slow concentration, as were her movements as she bent over and then straightened up again. Her face as it was then has been overlaid in my memory by the faces she had later. If I see her in my mind's eye as she was then, she doesn't have a face at all, and I have to reconstruct it. High forehead, high cheekbones, pale blue eyes, full lips that formed a perfect curve without any indentation, square chin. A broad-planed, strong, womanly face. I know that I found it beautiful. But I cannot recapture its beauty.

"*W*AIT," SHE said as I got up to go. "I have to leave too, and I'll walk with you.

I waited in the hall while she changed her clothes in the kitchen. The door was open a crack. She took off the smock and stood there in a bright green slip. Two stockings were hanging over the back of the chair. Picking one up, she gathered it into a roll using one hand, then the other, then balanced on one leg as she rested the heel of her other foot against her knee, leaned forward, slipped the rolled-up stocking over the tip of her foot, put her foot on the chair as she smoothed the stocking up over her calf, knee, and thigh, then bent to one side as she fastened the stocking to the garter belt. Straightening up, she took her foot off the chair and reached for the other stocking.

I couldn't take my eyes off her. Her neck and shoulders, her breasts, which the slip veiled rather than concealed, her hips which stretched the slip tight as she propped her foot on her knee and then set it on the chair, her leg, pale and naked, then shimmering in the silky stocking.

She felt me looking at her. As she was reaching for the other stocking, she paused, turned towards the door, and looked straight at me. I can't describe what kind of look it was—surprised, skeptical, knowing, reproachful. I turned red. For a fraction of a second I stood there, my face burning. Then I couldn't take it any more. I fled out of the apartment, down the stairs, and into the street.

I dawdled along. Bahnhofstrasse, Häusserstrasse, Blumenstrasse—it had been my way to school for years. I knew every building, every garden, and every fence, the ones that were repainted every year and the ones that were so gray and rotten that I could crumble the wood in my hand, the iron railings that I ran along as a child banging a stick against the posts and the high brick wall behind which I had imagined wonderful and terrible things, until I was able to climb it, and see row after boring row of neglected beds of flowers, berries, and vegetables. I knew the cobblestones in their layer of tar on the road, and the changing surface of the sidewalk, from flagstones to little lumps of basalt set in wave patterns, tar, and gravel.

It was all familiar. When my heart stopped pounding and my face was no longer scarlet, the encounter between the kitchen and the hall seemed a long way away. I was angry with myself. I had run away like a child, instead of keeping control of the situation, as I thought I should. I wasn't nine years old anymore, I was fifteen. That didn't mean I had any idea what keeping control would have entailed.

The other puzzle was the actual encounter that had taken place between the kitchen and the hall. Why had I not been able to take my eyes off her? She had a very strong, feminine body, more voluptuous than the girls I liked and watched. I was sure I wouldn't even have noticed her if I'd seen her at the swimming pool. Nor had she been any more naked than the girls and women I had already seen at the swimming pool. And besides, she was much older than the girls I dreamed about. Over thirty? It's hard to guess ages when you're not that old yourself and won't be anytime soon.

Years later it occurred to me that the reason I hadn't been able to take my eyes off her was not just her body, but the way she held herself and moved. I asked my girlfriends to put on stockings, but I didn't want to explain why, or to talk about the riddle of what had happened between the kitchen and the hall. So my request was read as a desire for garters and high heels and erotic extravaganza, and if it was granted, it was done as a come-on. There had been none of that when I had found myself unable to look away. She hadn't been posing or teasing me. I don't remember her ever doing that. I remember that her body and the way she held it and moved sometimes seemed awkward. Not that she was particularly heavy. It was more as if she had withdrawn into her own body, and left it to itself and its own quiet rhythms, unbothered by any input from her mind, oblivious to the outside world. It was the same obliviousness that weighed in her glance and her movements when she was pulling on her stockings. But then she was not awkward, she was slow-flowing, graceful, seductive—a seductiveness that had nothing to do with breasts and hips and legs, but was an invitation to forget the world in the recesses of the body.

I knew none of this—if indeed I know any of it now and am not just making patterns in the air. But as I thought back then on what had excited me, the excitement came back. To solve the riddle, I made myself remember the whole encounter, and then the distance I had created by turning it into a riddle dissolved, and I saw it all again, and again I couldn't take my eyes off her.

CHAPTER FIVE

A WEEK LATER I was standing at her door again.

For a week I had tried not to think about her. But I had nothing else to occupy or distract me; the doctor was not ready to let me go back to school, I was bored stiff with books after months of reading, and although friends still came to see me, I had been sick for so long that their visits could no longer bridge the gap between their daily lives and mine, and became shorter and shorter. I was supposed to go for walks, a little further each day, without overexerting myself. I could have used the exertion.

Being ill when you are a child or growing up is such an enchanted interlude! The outside world, the world of free time in the yard or the garden or on the street, is only a distant murmur in the sickroom. In-

side, a whole world of characters and stories prolif-
erates out of the books you read. The fever that
weakens your perception as it sharpens your imagination turns the sickroom into someplace new, both
familiar and strange; monsters come grinning out of
the patterns on the curtains and the carpet, and
chairs, tables, bookcases, and wardrobes burst out of
their normal shapes and become mountains and
buildings and ships you can almost touch although
they're far away. Through the long hours of the
night you have the church clock for company and
the rumble of the occasional passing car that throws
its headlights across the walls and ceiling. These are
hours without sleep, which is not to say that they're
sleepless, because on the contrary, they're not about
lack of anything, they're rich and full. Desires, memories, fears, passions form labyrinths in which we
lose and find and then lose ourselves again. They are
hours when anything is possible, good or bad.

This passes as you get better. But if the illness has
lasted long enough, the sickroom is impregnated
with it and although you're convalescing and the
fever has gone, you are still trapped in the labyrinth.

I awoke every day feeling guilty, sometimes with
my pajama pants damp or stained. The images and
scenes in my dreams were not right. I knew I would
not be scolded by my mother, or the pastor who had
instructed me for my confirmation and whom I admired, or by my older sister who was the confidante

of all my childhood secrets. But they would lecture me with loving concern, which was worse than being scolded. It was particularly wrong that when I was not just idly dreaming, I actively fantasized images and scenes.

I don't know where I found the courage to go back to Frau Schmitz. Did my moral upbringing somehow turn against itself? If looking at someone with desire was as bad as satisfying the desire, if having an active fantasy was as bad as the act you were fantasizing—then why not the satisfaction and the act itself? As the days went on, I discovered that I couldn't stop thinking sinful thoughts. In which case I also wanted the sin itself.

There was another way to look at it. Going there might be dangerous. But it was obviously impossible for the danger to act itself out. Frau Schmitz would greet me with surprise, listen to me apologize for my strange behavior, and amicably say goodbye. It was more dangerous not to go; I was running the risk of becoming trapped in my own fantasies. So I was doing the right thing by going. She would behave normally, I would behave normally, and everything would be normal again.

That is how I rationalized it back then, making my desire an entry in a strange moral accounting, and silencing my bad conscience. But that was not what gave me the courage to go to Frau Schmitz. It was one thing to tell myself that my mother, my admired pastor, and my older sister would not try to stop me if they really thought about it, but would in fact insist that I go. Actually going was something else again. I don't know why I did it. But today I can recognize that events back then were part of a life-long pattern in which thinking and doing have either come together or failed to come together—I think, I reach a conclusion, I turn the conclusion into a decision, and then I discover that acting on the decision is something else entirely, and that doing so may proceed from the decision, but then again it may not. Often enough in my life I have done things I had not decided to do. Something—whatever that may be—goes into action; "it" goes to the woman I don't want to see anymore, "it" makes the remark to the boss that costs me my head, "it" keeps on smoking although I have decided to quit, and then quits smoking just when I've accepted the fact that I'm a smoker and always will be. I don't mean to say that thinking and reaching decisions have no influence on behavior. But behavior does not merely enact whatever has already been thought through and decided. It has its own sources, and is my behavior, quite independently, just as my thoughts are my thoughts, and my decisions my decisions.

CHAPTER SIX

*S*HE WASN'T at home. The front door of the building stood ajar, so I went up the stairs, rang the bell, and waited. Then I rang again. Inside the apartment the doors were open, as I could see through the glass of the front door, and I could also make out the mirror, the wardrobe, and the clock in the hall. I could hear it ticking.

I sat down on the stairs and waited. I wasn't relieved, the way you can sometimes be when you feel funny about a certain decision and afraid of the consequences and then relieved that you've managed to carry out the former without incurring the latter. Nor was I disappointed. I was determined to see her and to wait until she came.

The clock in the hall struck the quarter hour, then the half hour, then the hour. I tried to follow its soft

ticking and to count the nine hundred seconds between one stroke and the next, but I kept losing
track. The yard buzzed with the sound of the carpenter's saws, the building echoed with voices or
music from one of the apartments, and a door
opened and closed. Then I heard slow, heavy, regular footsteps coming up the stairs. I hoped that whoever he was, he lived on the second floor. If he saw
me—how would I explain what I was doing there?
But the footsteps didn't stop at the second floor.
They kept coming. I stood up.

It was Frau Schmitz. In one hand she was carry-
ing a coal scuttle, in the other a box of briquets. She
was wearing a uniform jacket and skirt, and I realized that she was a streetcar conductor. She didn't
notice me until she reached the landing—she didn't
look annoyed, or surprised, or mocking—none of
the things I had feared. She looked tired. When she
put down the coke and was hunting in her jacket
pocket for the key, coins fell out onto the floor. I
picked them up and gave them to her.

"There are two more scuttles down in the cellar.
Will you fill them and bring them up? The door's
open."

I ran down the stairs. The door to the cellar was
open, the light was on, and at the bottom of the long
cellar stairs I found a bunker made of boards with
the door on the latch and a loose padlock hanging
from the open bolt. It was a large space, and the

coke was piled all the way up to the ceiling hatch through which it had been poured from the street into the cellar. On one side of the door was a neat stack of briquets; on the other side were the coal scuttles.

I don't know what I did wrong. At home I also fetched the coke from the cellar and never had any problems. But then the coke at home wasn't piled so high. Filling the first scuttle went fine. As I picked up the second scuttle by the handles and tried to shovel the coke up off the floor, the mountain began to move. From the top little pieces started bouncing down while the larger ones followed more sedately; further down it all began to slide and there was a general rolling and shifting on the floor. Black dust rose in clouds. I stood there, frightened, as the lumps came down and hit me and soon I was up to my ankles in coke.

I got my feet out of the coke, filled the second scuttle, looked for a broom, and when I found it I swept the lumps that had rolled out into the main part of the cellar back into the bunker, latched the door, and carried the two scuttles upstairs.

She had taken off her jacket, loosened her tie and undone the top button, and was sitting at the kitchen table with a glass of milk. She saw me, began to choke with laughter, and then let it out in full-throated peals. She pointed at me and slapped her other hand on the table. "Look at you, kid, just look at you!" Then I caught sight of my black face in the mirror over the sink, and laughed too.

"You can't go home like that. I'll run you a bath and beat the dust out of your clothes." She went to the tub and turned on the faucet. The water ran steaming into the tub. "Take your clothes off carefully, I don't need black dust all over the kitchen."

I hesitated, took off my sweater and shirt, and hesitated again. The water was rising quickly and the tub was almost full.

"Do you want to take a bath in your shoes and pants? I won't look, kid." But when I had turned off the faucet and taken off my underpants, she looked me over calmly. I turned red, climbed into the tub, and submerged myself. When I came up again she was out on the balcony with my clothes. I heard her beating the shoes against each other and shaking out my pants and sweater. She called down something about coal dust and sawdust, someone called back up to her, and she laughed. Back in the kitchen, she put my things on the chair. Glancing quickly at me, she said, "Take the shampoo and wash your hair. I'll bring a towel in a minute," then took something out of the wardrobe, and left the kitchen.

I washed myself. The water in the tub was dirty and I ran in some fresh so that I could wash my head and face clean under the flow. Then I lay there, listening to the boiler roar, and feeling the cool air on my face as it came through the half-open kitchen

door, and the warm water on my body. I was comfortable. It was an exciting kind of comfort and I got
hard.

I didn't look up when she came into the kitchen,
until she was standing by the tub. She was holding a
big towel in her outstretched arms. "Come!" I
turned my back as I stood up and climbed out of the
tub. From behind, she wrapped me in the towel
from head to foot and rubbed me dry. Then she let
the towel fall to the floor. I didn't dare move. She
came so close to me that I could feel her breasts
against my back and her stomach against my behind.
She was naked too. She put her arms around me, one
hand on my chest and the other on my erection.

"That's why you're here!"

"I . . ." I didn't know what to say. Not yes, but not
no either. I turned around. I couldn't see much of
her, we were standing too close. But I was over-
whelmed by the presence of her naked body. "You're
so beautiful!"

"Come on, kid, what are you talking about!" She
laughed and wrapped her arms around my neck. I
put my arms around her too.

I was afraid: of touching, of kissing, afraid I
wouldn't please her or satisfy her. But when we had
held each other for a while, when I had smelled her
smell and felt her warmth and her strength, everything fell into place. I explored her body with my
hands and mouth, our mouths met, and then she was

on top of me, looking into my eyes until I came and closed my eyes tight and tried to control myself and then screamed so loud that she had to cover my mouth with her hand to smother the sound.

CHAPTER SEVEN

HE NEXT night I fell in love with her. I could barely sleep, I was yearning for her, I dreamed of her, thought I could feel her until I realized that I was clutching the pillow or the blanket. My mouth hurt from kissing. I kept getting erections, but I didn't want to masturbate. I wanted to be with her.

Did I fall in love with her as the price for her having gone to bed with me? To this day, after spending the night with a woman, I feel I've been indulged and I must make it up somehow—to her by trying at least to love her, and to the world by facing up to it.

One of my few vivid recollections of early childhood has to do with a winter morning when I was four years old. The room I slept in at that time was unheated, and at night and first thing in the morning it was often very cold. I remember the warm kitchen and the hot stove, a heavy piece of iron equipment in which you could see the fire when you lifted out the plates and rings with a hook, and which always held a basin of hot water ready. My mother had pushed a chair up close to the stove for me to stand on while she washed and dressed me. I remember the wonderful feeling of warmth, and how good it felt to be washed and dressed in this warmth. I also remember that whenever I thought back to this afterwards, I always wondered why my mother had been spoiling me like this. Was I ill? Had my brothers and sisters been given something I hadn't? Was there something coming later in the day that was nasty or difficult that I had to get through?

Because the woman who didn't yet have a name in my mind had so spoiled me that afternoon, I went back to school the next day. It was also true that I wanted to show off my new manliness. Not that I would ever have talked about it. But I felt strong and superior, and I wanted to show off these feelings to the other kids and the teachers. Besides, I hadn't talked to her about it but I assumed that being a streetcar conductor she often had to work evenings and nights. How would I see her every day if I had to stay home and wasn't allowed to do anything except my convalescent walks?

When I came home from her, my parents and brother and sisters were already eating dinner.

"Why are you so late? Your mother was worried about you." My father sounded more annoyed than concerned.

I said that I'd lost my way, that I'd wanted to walk through the memorial garden in the cemetery to Molkenkur, but wandered around who knows where for a long time and ended up in Nussloch. "I had no money, so I had to walk home from Nussloch."

"You could have hitched a ride." My younger sister sometimes did this, but my parents disapproved.

My older brother snorted contemptuously. "Molkenkur and Nussloch are in completely opposite directions."

My older sister gave me a hard look.

"I'm going back to school tomorrow."

"So pay attention in Geography. There's north and there's south, and the sun rises . . ."

My mother interrupted my brother. "The doctor said another three weeks."

"If he can get all the way across the cemetery to Nussloch and back, he can also go to school. It's not his strength he's lacking, it's his brains." As small boys, my brother and I beat up on each other constantly, and later we fought with words. He was three years older than me, and better at both. At a certain point I stopped fighting back and let his attacks dissipate into thin air. Since then he had confined himself to grousing at me.

"What do you think?" My mother turned to my father. He set his knife and fork down on his plate, leaned back, and folded his hands in his lap. He said nothing and looked thoughtful, the way he always did when my mother talked to him about the children or the household. As usual, I wondered whether he was really turning over my mother's question in his mind, or whether he was thinking about work. Maybe he did try to think about my mother's question, but once his mind started going, he could only think about work. He was a professor of philosophy, and thinking was his life—thinking and reading and writing and teaching.

Sometimes I had the feeling that all of us in his family were like pets to him. The dog you take for a walk, the cat you play with and that curls up in your lap, purring, to be stroked—you can be fond of them, you can even need them to a certain extent, and nonetheless the whole thing—buying pet food, cleaning up the cat box, and trips to the vet—is really too much. Your life is elsewhere. I wish that we, his family, had been his life. Sometimes I also wished that my grousing brother and my cheeky little sister were different. But that evening I suddenly loved them all. My little sister. It probably wasn't easy being the youngest of four, and she needed to be cheeky just to hold her own. My older brother. We shared a bedroom, which must be even harder for him than it was for me, and on top of that, since I'd been ill he'd had to let me have the room to myself and sleep on the sofa in the living room. How could he not nag me? My father. Why should we children be his whole life? We were growing up and soon we'd be adults and out of the house.

I felt as if we were sitting all together for the last time around the round table under the five-armed, five-candled brass chandelier, as if we were eating our last meal off the old plates with the green vine-leaf border, as if we would never talk to each other so intimately again. I felt as if I were saying goodbye. I was still there and already gone. I was homesick for my mother and father and my brother and sisters, and I longed to be with the woman.

My father looked over at me. " 'I'm going back to school tomorrow'—that's what you said, isn't it?"

"Yes." So he had noticed that it was him I'd asked and not my mother, and also that I had not said I was wondering whether I should go back to school or not.

He nodded. "Let's have you go back to school. If it gets to be too much for you, you'll just stay home again."

I was pleased. And at the same time I felt I'd just said my final goodbyes.

CHAPTER EIGHT

*F*OR THE next few days, the woman was working the early shift. She came home at noon, and I cut my last class every day so as to be waiting for her on the landing outside her apartment. We showered and made love, and just before half past one I scrambled into my clothes and ran out the door. Lunch was at one-thirty. On Sundays lunch was at noon, but her early shift also started and ended later.

I would have preferred to skip the shower. She was scrupulously clean, she showered every morning, and I liked the smell of perfume, fresh perspiration, and streetcar that she brought with her from work. But I also liked her wet, soapy body; I liked to let her soap me and I liked to soap her, and she taught me not to do it bashfully, but with assurance and possessive thoroughness. When we made love, too, she took possession of me as a matter of course. Her mouth took mine, her tongue played with my tongue, she told me where to touch her and how, and when she rode me until she came, I was there only because she took pleasure in me and on me. I don't mean to say that she lacked tenderness and didn't give me pleasure. But she did it for her own playful enjoyment, until I learned to take possession of her too.

That came later. I never completely mastered it. And for a long time I didn't miss it. I was young, and I came quickly, and when I slowly came back alive again afterwards, I liked to have her take possession of me. I would look at her when she was on top of me, her stomach which made a deep crease above her navel, her breasts, the right one the tiniest bit larger than the left, her face and open mouth. She would lean both hands against my chest and throw them up at the last moment, as she gave a toneless sobbing cry that frightened me the first time, and that later I eagerly awaited.

Afterwards we were exhausted. She often fell asleep on top of me. I would listen to the saws in the yard and the loud cries of the workers who operated them and had to shout to make themselves heard. When the saws fell silent, the sound of the traffic echoed faintly in the kitchen. When I heard children calling and playing, I knew that school was out and that it was past one o'clock. The neighbor who came home at lunchtime scattered birdseed on his balcony, and the doves came and cooed.

"What's your name?" I asked her on the sixth or seventh day. She had fallen asleep on me and was just waking up. Until then I avoided saying anything to her that required me to choose either the formal or the familiar form of address.

She stared. "What?"

"What's your name?"

"Why do you want to know?" She looked at me suspiciously.

"You and I . . . I know your last name, but not your first. I want to know your first name. What's the matter with . . ."

She laughed. "Nothing, kid, there's nothing wrong with that. My name is Hanna." She kept on laughing, didn't stop, and it was contagious.

"You looked at me so oddly."

"I was still half asleep. What's yours?"

I thought she knew. At that time it was the in thing not to carry your schoolbooks in a bag but under your arm, and when I put them on her kitchen table, my name was on the front. But she hadn't paid any attention to them.

"My name is Michael Berg."

"Michael, Michael, Michael." She tried out the name. "My kid's called Michael, he's in college."

"In high school."

"In high school, he's what, seventeen?"

I was proud at the two extra years she'd given me, and nodded.

"He's seventeen and when he grows up he wants to be a famous . . ." She hesitated.

"I don't know what I want to be."

"But you study hard."

"Sort of." I told her she was more important to me than school and my studies. And I wished I were with her more often. "I'll have to repeat a class in any case."

"What class?" It was the first real conversation we'd had with each other.

"Tenth grade. I've missed too much in the last months while I was ill. If I still wanted to move up next year I'd have to work like an idiot. I'd also have to be in school right now." I told her I was cutting classes.

"Out." She threw back the coverlet. "Get out of my bed. And if you don't want to do your work, don't come back. Your work is idiotic? Idiotic? What do you think selling and punching tickets is?" She got out of bed, stood naked in the kitchen being a conductor. With her left hand she opened the little holder with the blocks of tickets, using her left thumb, covered with a rubber thimble, to pull off two tickets, flipped her right hand to get hold of the punch that hung from her wrist, and made two holes. "Two to Rohrbach." She dropped the punch, reached out her hand for a bill, opened the purse at her waist, put the money in, snapped it shut again, and squeezed the change out of the coin holder that was attached to it. "Who still doesn't have a ticket?" She looked at me. "Idiotic—you don't know what idiotic is."

I sat on the edge of the bed. I was stunned. "I'm sorry. I'll do my work. I don't know if I'll make it, school only has another six weeks to go. I'll try. But I won't get through it if I can't see you anymore." I . . ." At first I wanted to say, I love you. But then I didn't. Maybe she was right, of course she was right. But she had no right to demand that I do more at school, and make that the condition for our seeing each other again. "I can't not see you."

The clock in the hall struck one-thirty. "You have to go." She hesitated. "From tomorrow on I'm work-ing the main shift. I'll be home at five-thirty and you can come. Provided you work first."

We stood facing each other naked, but she couldn't have seemed more dismissive if she'd had on her uniform. I didn't understand what was going on. Was she thinking of me? Or of herself? If my schoolwork is idiotic, that makes her work even more so—that's what upset her? But I hadn't ever said that my work or hers was idiotic. Or was it that she didn't want a failure for a lover? But was I her lover? What was I to her? I dressed, dawdling, and hoped she would say something. But she said nothing. Then I had all my clothes on and she was still standing there naked, and as I kissed her good-bye, she didn't respond.

CHAPTER NINE

*W*HY DOES it make me so sad when I think back to that time? Is it yearning for past happiness—for I was happy in the weeks that followed, in which I really did work like a lunatic and passed the class, and we made love as if nothing else in the world mattered. Is it the knowledge of what came later, and that what came out afterwards had been there all along?

Why? Why does what was beautiful suddenly shatter in hindsight because it concealed dark truths? Why does the memory of years of happy marriage turn to gall when our partner is revealed to have had a lover all those years? Because such a situation makes it impossible to be happy? But we were happy! Sometimes the memory of happiness cannot stay true because it ended unhappily. Because happi-

ness is only real if it lasts forever? Because things always end painfully if they contained pain, conscious
or unconscious, all along? But what is unconscious,
unrecognized pain?

I think back to that time and I see my former self.
I wore the well-cut suits which had come down to
me from a rich uncle, now dead, along with several
pairs of two-tone shoes, black and brown, black and
white, suede and calf. My arms and legs were too
long, not for the suits, which my mother had let
down for me, but for my own movements. My
glasses were a cheap over-the-counter pair and my
hair a tangled mop, no matter what I did. In school I
was neither good nor bad; I think that many of the
teachers didn't really notice me, nor did the students
who dominated the class. I didn't like the way I
looked, the way I dressed and moved, what I
achieved and what I felt I was worth. But there was
so much energy in me, such belief that one day I'd be
handsome and clever and superior and admired,
such anticipation when I met new people and new
situations. Is that what makes me sad? The eagerness
and belief that filled me then and exacted a pledge
from life that life could never fulfill? Sometimes I see
the same eagerness and belief in the faces of children
and teenagers and the sight brings back the same
sadness I feel in remembering myself. Is this what
sadness is all about? Is it what comes over us when
beautiful memories shatter in hindsight because the

remembered happiness fed not just on actual circumstances but on a promise that was not kept?

She—I should start calling her Hanna, just as I started calling her Hanna back then—she certainly didn't nourish herself on promises, but was rooted in the here and now.

I asked her about her life, and it was as if she rummaged around in a dusty chest to get me the answers. She had grown up in a German community in Rumania, then come to Berlin at the age of sixteen, taken a job at the Siemens factory, and ended up in the army at twenty-one. Since the end of the war, she had done all manner of jobs to get by. She had been a streetcar conductor for several years; what she liked about the job was the uniform and the constant motion, the changing scenery and the wheels rolling under her feet. But that was all she liked about it. She had no family. She was thirty-six. She told me all this as if it were not her life but somebody else's, someone she didn't know well and who wasn't important to her. Things I wanted to know more about had vanished completely from her mind, and she didn't understand why I was interested in what had happened to her parents, whether she had had brothers and sisters, how she had lived in Berlin and what she'd done in the army. "The things you ask, kid!"

It was the same with the future—of course I wasn't hammering out plans for marriage and fu-

ture. But I identified more with Julien Sorel's relationship with Madame de Renal than his one with
Mathilde de la Mole. I was glad to see Felix Krull
end up in the arms of the mother rather than the
daughter. My sister, who was studying German literature, delivered a report at the dinner table about the
controversy as to whether Mr. von Goethe and
Madame von Stein had had a relationship, and I vigorously defended the idea, to the bafflement of my
family. I imagined how our relationship might be in
five or ten years. I asked Hanna how she imagined it.
She didn't even want to think ahead to Easter, when
I wanted to take a bicycle trip with her during the
vacation. We could get a room together as mother
and son, and spend the whole night together.

Strange that this idea and suggesting it were not
embarrassing to me. On a trip with my mother I
would have fought to get a room of my own. Having
my mother with me when I went to the doctor or to
buy a new coat or to be picked up by her after a trip
seemed to me to be something I had outgrown. If we
went somewhere together and we ran into my
schoolmates, I was afraid they would think I was a
mama's boy. But to be seen with Hanna, who was ten
years younger than my mother but could have been
my mother, didn't bother me. It made me proud.

When I see a woman of thirty-six today, I find her
young. But when I see a boy of fifteen, I see a child. I
am amazed at how much confidence Hanna gave

me. My success at school got my teachers' attention
and assured me of their respect. The girls I met noticed and liked it that I wasn't afraid of them. I felt at
ease in my own body.

The memory that illuminates and fixes my first
meetings with Hanna makes a single blur of the
weeks between our first conversation and the end of
the school year. One reason for that is we saw each
other so regularly and our meetings always followed
the same course. Another is that my days had never
been so full and my life had never been so swift and
so dense. When I think about the work I did in those
weeks, it's as if I had sat down at my desk and stayed
there until I had caught up with everything I'd
missed during my hepatitis, learned all the vocabu-
lary, read all the texts, worked through all the theo-
rems and memorized the periodic table. I had already
done the reading about the Weimar Republic and the
Third Reich while I was in my sickbed. And I remember our meetings in those weeks as one single
long meeting. After our conversation, they were always in the afternoon: if she was on the late shift,
then from three to four-thirty, otherwise until five-
thirty. Dinner was at seven, and at first Hanna forced
me to be home on time. But after a while an hour and
a half was not enough, and I began to think up ex-
cuses to miss dinner.

It all happened because of reading aloud. The day
after our conversation, Hanna wanted to know what

I was learning in school. I told her about Homer, Cicero, and Hemingway's story about the old man and his battle with the fish and the sea. She wanted to hear what Greek and Latin sounded like, and I read to her from the *Odyssey* and the speeches against Cataline.

"Are you also learning German?"

"How do you mean?"

"Do you only learn foreign languages, or is there still stuff you have to learn in your own?"

"We read texts." While I was sick, the class had read *Emilia Galotti* and *Intrigues and Love,* and there was an essay due on them. So I had to read both, which I did after finishing everything else. By then it was late, and I was tired, and next day I'd forgotten it all and had to start all over again.

"So read it to me!"

"Read it yourself, I'll bring it for you."

"You have such a nice voice, kid, I'd rather listen to you than read it myself."

"Oh, come on."

But next day when I arrived and wanted to kiss her, she pulled back. "First you have to read."

She was serious. I had to read *Emilia Galotti* to her for half an hour before she took me into the shower and then to bed. Now I enjoyed showering too—the desire I felt when I arrived had got lost as I read aloud to her. Reading a play out loud so that the various characters are more or less recognizable and come to life takes a certain concentration. Lust reasserted itself under the shower. So reading to her, showering with her, making love to her, and lying next to her for a while afterwards—that became the ritual in our meetings.

She was an attentive listener. Her laugh, her sniffs of contempt, and her angry or enthusiastic remarks left no doubt that she was following the action intently, and that she found both Emilia and Luise to be silly little girls. Her impatience when she sometimes asked me to go on reading seemed to come from the hope that all this imbecility would eventually play itself out. "Unbelievable!" Sometimes this made even me eager to keep reading. As the days grew longer, I read longer, so that I could be in bed with her in the twilight. When she had fallen asleep lying on me, and the saw in the yard was quiet, and a blackbird was singing as the colors of things in the kitchen dimmed until nothing remained of them but lighter and darker shades of gray, I was completely happy.

O N T H E first day of Easter vacation, I got up at four. Hanna was working the early shift. She rode her bicycle to the streetcar depot at a quarter past four and was on the streetcar to Schwetzingen at four-thirty. On the way out, she'd told me, the streetcar was often empty. It only filled up on the return journey.

I got on at the second stop. The second car was empty; Hanna was standing in the first car close to the driver. I debated whether I should sit in the first or the second car, and decided on the second. It promised privacy, a hug, a kiss. But Hanna didn't come. She must have seen that I had been waiting at the stop and had got on. That's why the streetcar had stopped. But she stayed up with the driver, talking and joking. I could see them.

The streetcar passed one stop after another. No one was waiting to get on. The streets were empty. It was not yet sunrise, and under a colorless sky everything lay pale in the pale light: buildings, parked cars, the new leaves on the trees and first flowers on the shrubs, the gas tank, and the mountains in the distance. The streetcar was moving slowly; presumably the schedule was based both on stopping times and on the time between each stop, and so the speed of travel had to be slowed down when there were no actual stops. I was imprisoned in the slow-moving car. At first I sat, then I went and stood on the front platform and tried to impale Hanna with my stare; I wanted her to feel my eyes in her back. After some time she turned around and glanced at me. Then she went on talking to the driver. The journey continued. Once we'd passed Eppelheim the rails were no longer in the surface of the road, but laid alongside on a graveled embankment. The car accelerated, with the regular *clackety-clack* of a train. I knew that this stretch continued through various places and ended up in Schwetzingen. But I felt rejected, exiled from the real world in which people lived and worked and loved. It was as if I were condemned to ride forever in an empty car to nowhere.

Then I saw another stop, a shelter in the middle of open country. I pulled the cord the conductors used to signal the driver to stop or start. The streetcar stopped. Neither Hanna nor the driver looked back at me when they heard the bell. As I got off, I thought they were looking at me and laughing. But I wasn't sure. Then the streetcar moved on, and I looked after it until it headed down into a dip and disappeared behind a hill. I was standing between the embankment and the road, there were fields around me, and fruit trees, and further on a nursery with greenhouses. The air was cool, and filled with the twittering of birds. Above the mountains the pale sky shone pink.

The trip on the streetcar had been like a bad dream. If I didn't remember its epilogue so vividly, I would actually be tempted to think of it as a bad dream. Standing at the streetcar stop, hearing the birds and watching the sun come up was like an awakening. But waking from a bad dream does not necessarily console you. It can also make you fully aware of the horror you just dreamed, and even of the truth residing in that horror. I set off towards home in tears, and couldn't stop crying until I reached Eppelheim.

I walked all the way back. I tried more than once to hitch a ride. When I was halfway there, the streetcar passed me. It was full. I didn't see Hanna.

I was waiting for her on the landing outside her apartment at noon, miserable, anxious, and furious.

"Are you cutting school again?"

"I'm on vacation. What was going on this morning?"

She unlocked the door and I followed her into the apartment and into the kitchen.

"What do you mean, what was going on this morning?"

"Why did you behave as if you didn't know me? I wanted . . ."

"I behaved as if I didn't know you?" She turned around and stared at me coldly. "You didn't want to know me. Getting into the second car when you could see I was in the first."

"Why would I get up at four-thirty on my first day of vacation to ride to Schwetzingen? Just to surprise you, because I thought you'd be happy. I got into the second car . . ."

"You poor baby. Up at four-thirty, and on your vacation too."

I had never seen her sarcastic before. She shook her head.

"How should I know why you're going to Schwetzingen? How should I know why you choose not to know me? It's your business, not mine. Would you leave now?"

I can't describe how furious I was. "That's not fair, Hanna. You knew, you had to know that I only got in the car to be with you. How can you believe I didn't want to know you? If I didn't, I would not have got on at all."

"Oh, leave me alone. I already told you, what you do is your business, not mine." She had moved so that the kitchen table was between us; everything in her look, her voice, and her gestures told me I was an intruder and should leave.

I sat down on the sofa. She had treated me badly and I had wanted to call her on it. But I hadn't got through to her. Instead, she was the one who'd attacked me. And I became uncertain. Could she be right, not objectively, but subjectively? Could she have, must she have misunderstood me? Had I hurt her, unintentionally, against my will, but hurt her anyway?

"I'm sorry, Hanna. Everything went wrong. I didn't mean to upset you, but it looks . . ."

"It looks? You think it looks like you upset me? *You* don't have the power to upset me. And will you please go, finally? I've been working, I want to take a bath, and I want a little peace." She looked at me commandingly. When I didn't get up, she shrugged, turned around, ran water into the tub, and took off her clothes.

Then I stood up and left. I thought I was leaving for good. But half an hour later I was back at her door. She let me in, and I said the whole thing was my fault. I had behaved thoughtlessly, inconsiderately, unlovingly. I understood that she was upset. I understood that she wasn't upset because I couldn't upset her. I understood that I couldn't upset her, but that she simply couldn't allow me to behave that way to her. In the end, I was happy that she admitted I'd hurt her.

So she wasn't as unmoved and uninvolved as she'd been making out, after all.

"Do you forgive me?"

She nodded.

"Do you love me?"

She nodded again. "The tub is still full. Come, I'll bathe you."

Later I wondered if she had left the water in the tub because she knew I would come back. If she had taken her clothes off because she knew I wouldn't be able to get that out of my head and that it would bring me back. If she had just wanted to win a power game.

After we'd made love and were lying next to each other and I told her why I'd got into the second car and not the first, she teased me. "You want to do it with me in the streetcar too? Kid, kid!" It was as if the actual cause of our fight had been meaningless.

But its results had meaning. I had not only lost this fight. I had caved in after a short struggle when she threatened to send me away and withhold herself. In the weeks that followed I didn't fight at all. If she threatened, I instantly and unconditionally surrendered. I took all the blame. I admitted mistakes I hadn't made, intentions I'd never had. Whenever she turned cold and hard, I begged her to be good to me again, to forgive me and love me. Sometimes I had the feeling that she hurt herself when she turned cold and rigid. As if what she was yearning for was

the warmth of my apologies, protestations, and en-
treaties. Sometimes I thought she just bullied me.
But either way, I had no choice.

I couldn't talk to her about it. Talking about our
fights only led to more fighting. Once or twice I
wrote her letters. But she didn't react, and when I
asked her about them, she said, "Are you starting
that again?"

O T T H A T Hanna and I weren't happy again after the first day of Easter vacation. We were never happier than in those weeks of April. As sham as our first fight and indeed all our fights were, everything that enlarged our ritual of reading, showering, making love, and lying beside each other did us good. Besides which, she had trumped herself with her accusation that I hadn't wanted to know her. When I wanted to be seen with her, she couldn't raise any fundamental objections. "So it was you who didn't want to be seen with me"—she didn't want to have to listen to that. So the week after Easter we set off by bike on a four-day trip to Wimpfen, Amorbach, and Miltenberg.

I don't remember what I told my parents. That I was doing the trip with my friend Matthias? With a group? That I was going to visit a former classmate? My mother was probably worried, as usual, and my father probably found, as usual, that she should stop worrying. Hadn't I just passed the class, when nobody thought I could do it?

While I was sick, I hadn't spent any of my pocket money. But that wouldn't be enough if I wanted to pay for Hanna as well. So I offered to sell my stamp collection to the stamp dealer next to the Church of the Holy Spirit. It was the only shop that said on the door that it purchased collections. The salesman looked through my album and offered me sixty marks. I made him look at my showpiece, a straight-edged Egyptian stamp with a pyramid that was listed in the catalog for four hundred marks. He shrugged. If I cared that much about my collection, maybe I should hang on to it. Was I even allowed to be selling it? What did my parents say about it? I tried to bargain. If the stamp with the pyramid wasn't that valuable, I would just keep it. Then he could only give me thirty marks. So the stamp with the pyramid was valuable after all? In the end I got seventy marks. I felt cheated, but I didn't care.

I was not the only one with itchy feet. To my amazement, Hanna started getting restless days before we left. She went this way and that over what to take, and packed and repacked the saddlebag and rucksack I had got hold of for her. When I wanted to show her the route I had worked out on the map, she didn't want to look, or even hear about it. "I'm too excited already. You'll have worked it out right anyway, kid."

We set off on Easter Monday. The sun was shining and went on shining for four days. The mornings were cool and then the days warmed up, not too warm for cycling, but warm enough to have picnics. The woods were carpets of green, with yellow green, bright green, bottle green, blue green, and black green daubs, flecks, and patches. In the flatlands along the Rhine, the first fruit trees were already in bloom. In Odenwald the first forsythias were out.

Often we could ride side by side. Then we pointed out to each other the things we saw: the castle, the fisherman, the boat on the river, the tent, the family walking single file along the bank, the enormous American convertible with the top down. When we changed directions or roads, I had to ride ahead; she didn't want to have to bother with such things. Otherwise, when the traffic was too heavy, she sometimes rode behind me and sometimes vice versa. Her bike had covered spokes, pedals, and gears, and she wore a blue dress with a big skirt that fluttered in her wake. It took me some time to stop worrying that the skirt would get caught in the spokes or the gears and she would fall off. After that, I liked watching her ride ahead of me.

How I had looked forward to the nights. I had imagined that we would make love, go to sleep, wake up, make love again, go to sleep again, wake up again and so on, night after night. But the only time I woke up again was the first night. She lay with her back to me, I leaned over her and kissed her, and she turned on her back, took me into her and held me in her arms. "Kid, kid." Then I fell asleep on top of her. The other nights we slept right through, worn out by the cycling, the sun, and the wind. We made love in the mornings.

Hanna didn't just let me be in charge of choosing our direction and the roads to take. I was the one who picked out the inns where we spent the nights, registered us as mother and son while she just signed her name, and selected our food from the menu for both of us. "I like not having to worry about a thing for a change."

The only fight we had took place in Amorbach. I had woken up early, dressed quietly, and crept out of the room. I wanted to bring up breakfast and also see if I could find a flower shop open where I could get a rose for Hanna. I had left a note on the night table. "Good morning! Bringing breakfast, be right back," or words to that effect. When I returned, she was standing in the room, trembling with rage and white-faced.

"How could you go just like that?"

I put down the breakfast tray with the rose on it and wanted to take her in my arms. "Hanna."

"Don't touch me." She was holding the narrow leather belt that she wore around her dress; she took a step backwards and hit me across the face with it. My lip split and I tasted blood. It didn't hurt. I was horrorstruck. She swung again.

But she didn't hit me. She let her arm fall, dropped the belt, and burst into tears. I had never seen her cry. Her face lost all its shape. Wide-open eyes, wide-open mouth, eyelids swollen after the first tears, red blotches on her cheeks and neck. Her mouth was making croaking, throaty sounds like the toneless cry when we made love. She stood there looking at me through her tears.

I should have taken her in my arms. But I couldn't. I didn't know what to do. At home none of us cried like that. We didn't hit, not even with our hands, let alone a leather belt. We talked. But what was I supposed to say now?

She took two steps towards me, beat her fists against me, then clung to me. Now I could hold her. Her shoulders trembled, she knocked her forehead against my chest. Then she gave a deep sigh and snuggled into my arms.

"Shall we have breakfast?" She let go of me. "My God, kid, look at you." She fetched a wet towel and cleaned my mouth and chin. "And your shirt is covered with blood." She took off the shirt and my pants, and we made love.

"What was the matter? Why did you get so angry?" We were lying side by side, so satiated and content that I thought everything would be cleared up now.

"What was the matter, what was the matter—you always ask such silly questions. You can't just leave like that."

"But I left you a note . . ."

"Note?"

I sat up. The note was no longer on the night table where I had left it. I got to my feet, and searched next to the night table, and underneath, and under the bed and in it. I couldn't find it. "I don't understand. I wrote you a note saying I was going to get breakfast and I'd be right back."

"You did? I don't see any note."

"You don't believe me?"

"I'd love to believe you. But I don't see any note."

We didn't go on fighting. Had a gust of wind come and taken the note and carried it away to God knows where? Had it all been a misunderstanding, her fury, my split lip, her wounded face, my helplessness?

Should I have gone on searching, for the note, for the cause of Hanna's fury, for the source of my helplessness? "Read me something, kid!" She cuddled up to me and I picked up Eichendorff's *Memoirs of a Good-for-Nothing* and continued from where I had left off. *Memoirs of a Good-for-Nothing* was easy to read aloud, easier than *Emilia Galotti* and *Intrigues and Love*. Again, Hanna followed everything eagerly. She liked the scattering of poems. She liked the disguises, the mix-ups, the complications and pursuits which the hero gets tangled up in in Italy. At the same time, she held it against him that he's a good-for-nothing who doesn't achieve anything, can't do anything, and doesn't want to besides. She was torn in all directions; hours after I stopped reading, she was still coming up with questions. "Customs collector—wasn't much of a job?"

Once again the report on our fight has become so detailed that I would like to report on our happiness. The fight made our relationship more intimate. I had seen her crying. The Hanna who could cry was closer to me than the Hanna who was only strong. She began to show a soft side that I had never seen before. She kept looking at my split lip, until it healed, and stroking it gently.

We made love a different way. For a long time I had abandoned myself to her and her power of possession. Then I had also learned to take possession of her. On this trip and afterwards, we no longer merely took possession of each other.

I have a poem that I wrote back then. As poetry, it's worthless. At the time I was in love with Rilke and Benn, and I can see that I wanted to imitate them both. But I can also see how close we were at the time. Here is the poem:

> *When we open ourselves*
> *you yourself to me and I myself to you,*

when we submerge
you into me and I into you
when we vanish
into me you and into you I

Then
am I me
and you are you

CHAPTER TWELVE

*W*HILE I have no memory of the lies I told my parents about the trip with Hanna, I do remember the price I had to pay to stay alone at home the last week of vacation. I can't recall where my parents and my older brother and sister were going. The problem was my little sister. She was supposed to go and stay with a friend's family. But if I was going to be at home, she wanted to be at home as well. My parents didn't want that. So I was supposed to go and stay with a friend too.

As I look back, I find it remarkable that my parents were willing to leave me, a fifteen-year-old, at home alone for a week. Had they noticed the independence that had been growing in me since I met Hanna? Or had they simply registered the fact that I had passed the class despite the months of illness and decided that I was more responsible and trustworthy than I had shown myself to be until then? Nor do I remember being called on to explain the many hours I spent at Hanna's. My parents apparently believed that, now that I was healthy again, I wanted to be with my friends as much as possible, whether studying or just enjoying our free time. Besides, when parents have a pack of four children, their attention cannot cover everything, and tends to focus on whichever one is causing the most problems at the moment. I had caused problems for long enough; my parents were relieved that I was healthy and would be moving up into the next class.

When I asked my little sister what her price was for going to stay with her friend while I stayed home, she demanded jeans—we called them blue jeans back then, or studded pants—and a Nicki, which was a velour sweater. That made sense. Jeans were still something special at that time, they were chic, and they promised liberation from herringbone suits and big-flowered dresses. Just as I had to wear my uncle's things, my little sister had to wear her big sister's. But I had no money.

"Then steal them!" said my little sister with perfect equanimity.

It was astonishingly easy. I tried on various jeans, took a pair her size with me into the fitting room, and carried them out of the store against my stomach under my wide suit pants. The sweater I stole from the big main department store. My little sister and I went in one day and strolled from stand to stand in the fashion department until we found the right stand and the right sweater. Next day I marched quickly through the department, seized the sweater, hid it under my suit jacket, and was outside again. The day after that I stole a silk nightgown for Hanna, was spotted by the store detective, ran for my life, and escaped by a hair. I didn't go back to the department store for years after that.

Since our nights together on the trip, I had longed every night to feel her next to me, to curl up against her, my stomach against her behind and my chest against her back, to rest my hand on her breasts, to reach out for her when I woke up in the night, find her, push my leg over her legs, and press my face against her shoulder. A week alone at home meant seven nights with Hanna.

One evening I invited her to the house and cooked for her. She stood in the kitchen as I put the finishing touches on the food. She stood in the open double doors between the dining room and living room as I served. She sat at the round dining table where my father usually sat. She looked around.

Her eyes explored everything—the Biedermeier furniture, the piano, the old grandfather clock, the pictures, the bookcases, the plates and cutlery on the table. When I left her alone to prepare dessert, she was not at the table when I came back. She had gone from room to room and was standing in my father's study. I leaned quietly against the doorpost and watched her. She let her eyes drift over the bookshelves that filled the walls, as if she were reading a text. Then she went to a shelf, raised her right index finger chest high and ran it slowly along the backs of the books, moved to the next shelf, ran her finger further along, from one spine to the next, pacing off the whole room. She stopped at the window, looked out into the darkness, at the reflection of the bookshelves, and at her own.

It is one of the pictures of Hanna that has stayed with me. I have them stored away, I can project them on a mental screen and watch them, unchanged, unconsumed. There are long periods when I don't think about them at all. But they always come back into my head, and then I sometimes have to run them repeatedly through my mental projector and watch them. One is Hanna putting on her stockings in the kitchen. Another is Hanna standing in front of the tub holding the towel in her outstretched arms. Another is Hanna riding her bike with her skirt blowing in her slipstream. Then there is the picture of Hanna in my father's study. She's wearing a blue-and-white striped dress, what they called a shirtwaist back then. She looks young in it. She has run her finger along the backs of the books and looked into the darkness of the window. She turns to me, quickly enough that the skirt swings out around her legs for a moment before it hangs smooth again. Her eyes are tired.

"Are these books your father has just read, or did he write them too?"

I knew there was a book on Kant and another on Hegel that my father had written, and I searched for them and showed them to her.

"Read me something from them. Please, kid?"

"I . . ." I didn't want to, but didn't like to refuse her either. I took my father's Kant book and read her a passage on analysis and dialectics that neither of us understood. "Is that enough?"

She looked at me as though she had understood it all, or as if it didn't matter whether anything was understandable or not. "Will you write books like that some day?"

I shook my head.

"Will you write other books?"

"I don't know."

"Will you write plays?"

"I don't know, Hanna."

She nodded. Then we ate dessert and went to her apartment. I would have liked to sleep with her in my bed, but she didn't want to. She felt like an intruder in our house. She didn't say it in so many words, but in the way she stood in the kitchen or in the open double doors, or walked from room to room, inspected my father's books and sat with me at dinner.

I gave her the silk nightgown. It was aubergine-colored with narrow straps that left her shoulders and arms bare, and came down to her ankles. It shone and shimmered. Hanna was delighted; she laughed and beamed. She looked down at herself, turned around, danced a few steps, looked at herself in the mirror, checked her reflection, and danced some more. That too is a picture of Hanna that has stayed with me.

CHAPTER THIRTEEN

I ALWAYS EXPERIENCED the beginning
of a new school year as a watershed. Moving
up from tenth to eleventh grade was a major one. My
class was disbanded among the three other parallel
classes. Quite a few students had failed to make the
grade, so four small classes were combined into three
larger ones.

My high school traditionally had taken only boys.
When girls began to be accepted, there were so few
of them to begin with that they were not divided
equally among the parallel classes, but were assigned
to a single class, then later to a second and a third,
until they made up a third of each class. There were
not enough girls in my year for any to be assigned to
my former class. We were the fourth parallel class,
and all boys, which is why we were the ones to be

disbanded and reassigned, and not one of the other classes.

We didn't find out about it until school began. The principal summoned us into a classroom and informed us about the why and how of our reassignment. Along with six others, I crossed the empty halls to the new classroom. We got the seats that were left over; mine was in the second row. They were individual seats, but in pairs, divided into three rows. I was in the middle row. On my left I had a classmate from my old class, Rudolf Bargen, a heavyset, calm, dependable chess and hockey player with whom I hadn't ever spent any time in my old class, but who soon became a good friend. On my right, across the aisle, were the girls.

My neighbor was Sophie. Brown hair, brown eyes, brown summer skin, with tiny golden hairs on her bare arms. After I'd sat down and looked around, she smiled at me.

I smiled back. I felt good, I was excited about a new start in a new class, and the girls. I had observed my mates in tenth grade: whether they had girls in their class or not, they were afraid of them, or kept out of their way, or showed off to them, or worshipped them. I knew my way around women, and could be comfortable and open in a friendly way. The girls liked that. I would get along with them well in the new class, which meant I'd get along with the boys too.

Does everyone feel this way? When I was young,
I was perpetually overconfident or insecure. Either I
felt completely useless, unattractive, and worthless,
or that I was pretty much a success, and everything I
did was bound to succeed. When I was confident, I
could overcome the hardest challenges. But all it
took was the smallest setback for me to be sure that I
was utterly worthless. Regaining my self-confidence
had nothing to do with success; every goal I set myself, every recognition I craved made anything I actually did seem paltry by comparison, and whether I
experienced it as a failure or triumph was utterly de-
pendent on my mood. With Hanna things felt good
for weeks—in spite of our fights, in spite of the fact
that she pushed me away again and again, and again
and again I crawled to her. And so summer in the
new class began well.

I can still see the classroom: right front, the door,
along the right-hand wall the board with the clothes
hooks, on the left a row of windows looking onto the
Heiligenberg and—when we stood next to the glass
at recess—down at the streets, the river and the
meadows on the opposite bank; in front, the black-
board, the stands for maps and diagrams, and the
teacher's desk and chair on a foot-high platform.
The walls had yellow oil paint on them to about
head height, and above that, white; and from the
ceiling hung two milky glass globes. There was not
one superfluous thing in the room: no pictures, no

plants, no extra chair, no cupboard with forgotten books and notebooks and colored chalk. When your eyes wandered, they wandered to what was outside the window, or to whoever was sitting next to you. When Sophie saw me looking at her, she turned and smiled at me.

"Berg, Sophia may be a Greek name, but that is no reason for you to study your neighbor in a Greek lesson. Translate!"

We were translating the *Odyssey*. I had read it in German, loved it, and love it to this day. When it was my turn, it took me only seconds to find my place and translate. After the teacher had stopped teasing me about Sophie and the class had stopped laughing, it was something else that made me stutter. Nausicaa, white-armed and virginal, who in body and features resembled the immortals—should I imagine her as Hanna or as Sophie? It had to be one of the two.

CHAPTER FOURTEEN

WHEN AN airplane's engines fail, it is not the end of the flight. Airplanes don't fall out of the sky like stones. They glide on, the enormous multi-engined passenger jets, for thirty, forty-five minutes, only to smash themselves up when they attempt a landing. The passengers don't notice a thing. Flying feels the same whether the engines are working or not. It's quieter, but only slightly: the wind drowns out the engines as it buffets the tail and wings. At some point, the earth or sea look dangerously close through the window. But perhaps the movie is on, and the stewards and air hostesses have closed the shades. Maybe the very quietness of the flight is appealing to the passengers.

That summer was the glide path of our love. Or rather, of my love for Hanna. I don't know about her love for me.

We kept up our ritual of reading aloud, showering, making love, and then lying together. I read her *War and Peace* with all of Tolstoy's disquisitions on history, great men, Russia, love and marriage; it must have lasted forty or fifty hours. Again, Hanna became absorbed in the unfolding of the book. But it was different this time; she withheld her own opinions; she didn't make Natasha, Andrei, and Pierre part of her world, as she had Luise and Emilia, but entered their world the way one sets out on a long and dazzling journey, or enters a castle which one is allowed to visit, even stay in until one feels at home, but without ever really shedding one's inhibitions. All the things I had read to her before were already familiar to me. *War and Peace* was new for me, too. We took the long journey together.

We thought up pet names for each other. She began not just to call me Kid, but gave me other attributes and diminutives, such as Frog or Toad, Puppy, Toy, and Rose. I stuck to Hanna, until she asked me, "Which animal do you see when you hold me and close your eyes and think of animals?" I closed my eyes and thought of animals. We were lying snuggled close together, my head on her neck, my neck on her breasts, my right arm underneath her against her back and my left hand on her behind. I ran my arms and hands over her broad back, her hard thighs, her firm ass, and also felt the solidity of her breasts and stomach against my neck and chest.

Her skin was smooth and soft to the touch, the body beneath it strong and reliable. When my hand lay on her calf, I felt the constant twitching play of muscles. It reminded me of the way a horse twitches its hide to repel flies. "A horse."

"A horse?" She disentangled herself, sat up and stared at me, stared in shock.

"You don't like it? It came to me because you feel so good, smooth and soft and all firm and strong underneath. And because your calf twitches." I explained my association.

She looked at the ripple of the muscles in her calf. "Horse." She shook her head. "I don't know . . ."

That wasn't how she usually was. Usually she was absolutely single-minded, whether in agreement or disagreement. Faced with her look of shock, I had been ready to take it all back if necessary, blame myself, and apologize. But now I tried to reconcile her to the horse. "I could call you Cheval or Pony or Little Equus. When I think of horses, I don't think horse's teeth or horse face or whatever it is that worries you, I think of something good, warm, soft, strong. You're not a bunny or a kitten, and whatever there is in a tiger—that evil something—that's not you either."

She lay down on her back, arms behind her head. Now it was me who sat up to look at her. She was staring into space. After a while she turned her face to me. Her expression was curiously naked. "Yes, I like it when you call me Horse or those other horse names—can you explain them to me?"

Once we went to the theater in the next town to see Schiller's *Intrigues and Love.* It was the first time Hanna had been to the theater, and she loved all of it, from the performance to the champagne at intermission. I put my arm around her waist, and didn't care what people might think of us as a couple, and I was proud that I didn't care. At the same time, I knew that in the theater in our hometown I would care. Did she know that too?

She knew that my life that summer no longer revolved around her, and school, and my studies. More and more, when I came to her in the late afternoon, I came from the swimming pool. That was where our class got together, did our homework, played soccer and volleyball and skat, and flirted. That was where our class socialized, and it meant a lot to me to be part of it and to belong. The fact that I came later than the others or left earlier, depending on Hanna's schedule, didn't hurt my reputation, but made me interesting. I knew that. I also knew that I wasn't missing anything, and yet I often had the feeling that absolutely everything could be happening while I wasn't there. There was a long stretch when I did not dare ask myself whether I would rather be at the swimming pool or with Hanna. But on my birthday in July, there was a party for me at the pool, and it was hard to tear myself away from it when they didn't want me to go, and then an exhausted Hanna received me in a bad mood. She didn't know it was my birthday. When I had asked her about hers, and she had told me it was the twenty-first of October, she hadn't asked me when mine was. She was also no more bad-tempered than she always was when she was exhausted. But I was annoyed by her bad temper, and I wanted to be somewhere else, at the pool, away with my classmates, swept up in the exuberance of our talk, our banter, our games, and our flirtations. Then when I proceeded to get bad-tempered myself and we started a fight and Hanna treated me like a nonentity, the fear of losing her returned and I humbled myself and begged her pardon until she took me back. But I was filled with resentment.

CHAPTER FIFTEEN

$\mathcal{T}$HEN I began to betray her.

Not that I gave away any secrets or exposed Hanna. I didn't reveal anything that I should have kept to myself. I kept something to myself that I should have revealed. I didn't acknowledge her. I know that disavowal is an unusual form of betrayal. From the outside it is impossible to tell if you are disowning someone or simply exercising discretion, being considerate, avoiding embarrassments and sources of irritation. But you, who are doing the disowning, you know what you're doing. And disavowal pulls the underpinnings away from a relationship just as surely as other more flamboyant types of betrayal.

I no longer remember when I first denied Hanna. Friendships coalesced out of the casual ease of those summer afternoons at the swimming pool. Aside from the boy who sat next to me in school, whom I knew from the old class, the person I liked especially in the new class was Holger Schlüter, who like me was interested in history and literature, and with whom I quickly felt at ease. He also got along with Sophie, who lived a few blocks behind our house, which meant that we went to and from the swimming pool together. At first I told myself that I wasn't yet close enough to my friends to tell them about Hanna. Then I didn't find the right opportunity, the right moment, the right words. And finally it was too late to tell them about Hanna, to present her along with all my other youthful secrets. I told myself that talking about her so belatedly would misrepresent things, make it seem as if I had kept silent about Hanna for so long because our relationship wasn't right and I felt guilty about it. But no matter what I pretended to myself, I knew that I was betraying Hanna when I acted as if I was letting my friends in on everything important in my life but said nothing about Hanna.

The fact that they knew I wasn't being completely open only made things worse. One evening Sophie and I got caught in a thunderstorm on our way home and took shelter under the overhang of a garden shed in Neuenheimer Feld, which had no university buildings on it then, just fields and gardens. It thundered, the lightning crackled, the wind came in gusts, and rain fell in big heavy drops. At the same time the temperature dropped a good ten degrees. We were freezing, and I put my arm around her.

"You know . . ." She wasn't looking at me, but out at the rain.

"What?"

"You were sick with hepatitis for a long time. Is that what's on your mind? Are you afraid you won't really get well again? Did the doctors say something? And do you have to go to the clinic every day to get tests or transfusions?"

Hanna as illness. I was ashamed. But I really couldn't start talking about Hanna at this point. "No, Sophie, I'm not sick anymore. My liver is normal, and in a year I'll even be able to drink alcohol if I want, but I don't. What's . . ." Talking about Hanna, I didn't want to say "what's bothering me." "There's another reason I arrive later or leave earlier."

"Do you not want to talk about it, or is it that you want to but you don't know how?"

Did I not want to, or didn't I know how? I didn't know the answer. But as we stood there under the lightning, with the explosions of thunder rumbling almost overhead and the pounding of the rain, both freezing, warming each other a little, I had the feeling that I had to tell her, of all people, about Hanna. "Maybe I can tell you some other time."

But there never was another time.

CHAPTER SIXTEEN

I NEVER FOUND out what Hanna did when she wasn't working and we weren't to-gether. When I asked, she turned away my questions. We did not have a world that we shared; she gave me the space in her life that she wanted me to have. I had to be content with that. Wanting more, even wanting to know more, was presumption on my part. If we were particularly happy with each other and I asked her something because at that moment it felt as if everything was possible and allowed, then she some-times ducked my questions, instead of refusing out-right to answer them. "The things you ask, kid!" Or she would take my hand and lay it on her stomach. "Are you trying to make holes in me?" Or she would count on her fingers. "Laundry, ironing, sweeping, dusting, shopping, cooking, shake plums out of tree, pick up plums, bring plums home and cook them quick before the little one"—and here she would take hold of the fifth finger of her left hand between her right thumb and forefinger—"eats them all himself."

I never met her unexpectedly on the street or in a store or a movie theater, although she told me she loved going to the movies, and in our first months together I always wanted to go with her, but she wouldn't let me. Sometimes we talked about films we had both seen. She went no matter what was showing, and saw everything, from German war and folk movies to Westerns and New Wave films, and I liked what came out of Hollywood, whether it was set in ancient Rome or the Wild West. There was one Western in particular that we both loved: the one with Richard Widmark playing a sheriff who has to fight a duel next morning that he's bound to lose, and in the evening he knocks on Dorothy Malone's door—she's been trying, but failing, to get him to make a break for it. She opens up. "What do you want now? Your whole life in one night?" Sometimes Hanna teased me when I came to her full of desire, with "What do you want now? Your whole life in one hour?"

Only once did I ever see Hanna by chance. It was the end of July or the beginning of August, in the last few days before summer vacation.

Hanna had been behaving oddly for days, moody and peremptory, and at the same time palpably under some kind of pressure that was absolutely tormenting her and left her acutely sensitive and vulnerable. She pulled herself together and held herself tight as if to stop herself from exploding. When I asked what was upsetting her so, she snapped at me. That was hard for me to take. I felt rejected, but I also felt her helplessness, and I tried to be there for her and at the same time to leave her in peace. One day the pressure was gone. At first I thought Hanna was her usual self again. We had not started a new book after the end of *War and Peace,* but I had promised I'd see to it, and had brought several books to choose from.

But she didn't want that. "Let me bathe you, kid."

It wasn't summer's humidity that had settled on me like a heavy net when I came into the kitchen. Hanna had turned on the boiler for the bathwater. She filled the tub, put in a few drops of lavender oil, and washed me. She wore her pale blue flowered smock with no underwear underneath; the smock stuck to her sweating body in the hot, damp air. She excited me very much. When we made love, I sensed that she wanted to push me to the point of feeling things I had never felt before, to the point where I could no longer stand it. She also gave herself in a way she had never done before. She didn't abandon all reserve, she never did that. But it was as if she wanted us to drown together.

"Now go to your friends." She dismissed me, and I went. The heat stood solidly between the buildings, lay over the fields and gardens, and shimmered above the asphalt. I was numb. At the swimming pool the shrieks of playing, splashing children reached me as if from far, far away. I moved through the world as if it had nothing to do with me nor I with it. I dived into the milky chlorinated water and felt no compulsion to surface again. I lay near the others, listening to them, and found what they said silly and pointless.

Eventually the feeling passed. Eventually it turned into an ordinary afternoon at the swimming pool with homework and volleyball and gossip and flirting. I can't remember what it was I was doing when I looked up and saw her.

She was standing twenty or thirty meters away, in shorts and an open blouse knotted at the waist, looking at me. I looked back at her. She was too far away for me to read her expression. I didn't jump to my feet and run to her. Questions raced through my head: Why was she at the pool, did she want to be seen with me, did I want to be seen with her, why had we never met each other by accident, what should I do? Then I stood up. And in that briefest of moments in which I took my eyes off her, she was gone.

Hanna in shorts, with the tails of her blouse knotted, her face turned towards me but with an expression I cannot read at all—that is another picture I have of her.

CHAPTER SEVENTEEN

NEXT DAY she was gone. I came at the usual time and rang the bell. I looked through the door, everything looked the way it always did, I could hear the clock ticking.

I sat down on the stairs once again. During our first few months, I had always known what line she was working on, even though I had never repeated my attempt to accompany her or even pick her up afterwards. At some point I had stopped asking, stopped even wondering. It hadn't even occurred to me until now.

I used the telephone booth at the Wilhelmsplatz to call the streetcar company, was transferred from one person to the next, and finally was told that Hanna Schmitz had not come to work. I went back to Bahnhofstrasse, asked at the carpenter's shop in the yard for the name of the owner of the building, and got a name and address in Kirchheim. I rode over there.

"Frau Schmitz? She moved out this morning."

"And her furniture?"

"It's not her furniture."

"How long did she live in the apartment?"

"What's it to you?" The woman who had been talking to me through a window in the door slammed it shut.

In the administration building of the streetcar company, I talked my way through to the personnel department. The man in charge was friendly and concerned.

"She called this morning early enough for us to arrange for a substitute, and said that she wouldn't be coming back, period." He shook his head. "Two weeks ago she was sitting there in your chair and I offered to have her trained as a driver, and she throws it all away."

It took me some days to think of going to the citizens' registration office. She had informed them she was moving to Hamburg, but without giving an address.

The days went by and I felt sick. I took pains to make sure my parents and my brothers and sisters noticed nothing. I joined in the conversation at table a little, ate a little, and when I had to throw up, I managed to make it to the toilet. I went to school and to the swimming pool. I spent my afternoons there in an out-of-the-way place where no one would look for me. My body yearned for Hanna. But even worse than my physical desire was my sense of guilt. Why hadn't I jumped up immediately when she stood there and run to her! This one moment summed up all my halfheartedness of the past months, which had produced my denial of her, and my betrayal. Leaving was her punishment.

Sometimes I tried to tell myself that it wasn't her I had seen. How could I be sure it was her when I hadn't been able to make out the face? If it had been her, wouldn't I have had to recognize her face? So couldn't I be sure it wasn't her at all?

But I knew it was her. She stood and looked—and it was too late.

PART TWO

CHAPTER ONE

AFTER HANNA left the city, it took a while before I stopped watching for her everywhere, before I got used to the fact that afternoons had lost their shape, and before I could look at books and open them without asking myself whether they were suitable for reading aloud. It took a while before my body stopped yearning for hers; sometimes I myself was aware of my arms and legs groping for her in my sleep, and my brother reported more than once at table that I had called out "Hanna" in the night. I can also remember classes at school when I did nothing but dream of her, think of her. The feeling of guilt that had tortured me in the first weeks gradually faded. I avoided her building, took other routes, and six months later my family moved to another part of town. It wasn't that I forgot Hanna. But at a certain point the memory of her stopped accompanying me wherever I went. She stayed behind, the way a city stays behind as a train pulls out of the station. It's there, somewhere behind you, and you could go back and make sure of it. But why should you?

I remember my last years of school and my first years at university as happy. Yet I can't say very much about them. They were effortless; I had no difficulty with my final exams at school or with the legal studies that I chose because I couldn't think of anything else I really wanted to do; I had no difficulty with friendships, with relationships or the end of relationships—I had no difficulty with anything. Everything was easy; nothing weighed heavily. Perhaps that is why my bundle of memories is so small. Or do I keep it small? I also wonder if my memory of happiness is even true. If I think about it more, plenty of embarrassing and painful situations come to mind, and I know that even if I had said goodbye to my memory of Hanna, I had not overcome it. Never to let myself be humiliated or humiliate myself after Hanna, never to take guilt upon myself or feel guilty, never again to love anyone whom it would hurt to lose—I didn't formulate any of this as I thought back then, but I know that's how I felt.

I adopted a posture of arrogant superiority. I behaved as if nothing could touch or shake or confuse me. I got involved in nothing, and I remember a teacher who saw through this and spoke to me about it; I was arrogantly dismissive. I also remember Sophie. Not long after Hanna left the city, Sophie was diagnosed with tuberculosis. She spent three years in a sanitorium, returning just as I went to university. She felt lonely, and sought out contact with her old friends. It wasn't hard for me to find a way into her heart. After we slept together, she realized I wasn't interested in her; in tears, she asked, "What's happened to you, what's happened to you?" I remember my grandfather during one of my last visits before his death; he wanted to bless me, and I told him I didn't believe in any of that and didn't want it. It is hard for me to imagine that I felt good about behaving like that. I also remember that the smallest gesture of affection would bring a lump to my throat, whether it was directed at me or at someone else. Sometimes all it took was a scene in a movie. This juxtaposition of callousness and extreme sensitivity seemed suspicious even to me.

CHAPTER TWO

*W*HEN I saw Hanna again, it was in a courtroom.

It wasn't the first trial dealing with the camps, nor was it one of the major ones. Our professor, one of the few at that time who were working on the Nazi past and the related trials, made it the subject of a seminar, in the hope of being able to follow the entire trial with the help of his students, and evaluate it. I can no longer remember what it was he wanted to examine, confirm, or disprove. I do remember that we argued the prohibition of retroactive justice in the seminar. Was it sufficient that the ordinances under which the camp guards and enforcers were convicted were already on the statute books at the time they committed their crimes? Or was it a question of how the laws were actually interpreted and enforced at the time they committed their crimes, and that they were not applied to them? What is law? Is it what is on the books, or what is actually enacted and obeyed in a society? Or is law what must be enacted and obeyed, whether or not it is on the books, if things are to go right? The professor, an old gentleman who had returned from exile but remained an outsider among German legal scholars, participated in these debates with all the force of his scholarship, and yet at the same time with a detachment that no longer relied on pure scholarship to provide the solution to a problem. "Look at the defendants—you won't find a single one who really believes he had the dispensation to murder back then."

The seminar began in winter, the trial in spring. It lasted for weeks. The court was in session Mondays through Thursdays, and the professor assigned a group of students to keep a word-for-word record for each day. The seminar was held on Fridays, and explored the data gathered during the preceding week.

Exploration! Exploring the past! We students in the seminar considered ourselves radical explorers. We tore open the windows and let in the air, the wind that finally whirled away the dust that society had permitted to settle over the horrors of the past. We made sure people could breathe and see. And we placed no reliance on legal scholarship. It was evident to us that there had to be convictions. It was just as evident that conviction of this or that camp guard or enforcer was only the prelude. The generation that had been served by the guards and enforcers, or had done nothing to stop them, or had not banished them from its midst as it could have done after 1945, was in the dock, and we explored it, subjected it to trial by daylight, and condemned it to shame.

Our parents had played a variety of roles in the Third Reich. Several among our fathers had been in the war, two or three of them as officers of the Wehrmacht and one as an officer of the Waffen SS. Some of them had held positions in the judiciary or local government. Our parents also included teachers and doctors, and one of us had an uncle who had been a high official in the Ministry of the Interior. I am sure that to the extent that we asked and to the extent that they answered us, they had very different stories to tell. My father did not want to talk about himself, but I knew that he had lost his job as lecturer in philosophy for scheduling a lecture on Spinoza, and had got himself and us through the war as an editor for a house that published hiking maps and books. How did I decide that he too was under sentence of shame? But I did. We all condemned our parents to shame, even if the only charge we could bring was that after 1945 they had tolerated the perpetrators in their midst.

We students in the seminar developed a strong group identity. We were the students of the camps—that's how the other students described us, and how we soon came to call ourselves. What we were doing didn't interest the others; it alienated many of them, literally repelled some. When I think about it now, I think that our eagerness to assimilate the horrors and our desire to make everyone else aware of them was in fact repulsive. The more horrible the events about which we read and heard, the more certain we became of our responsibility to enlighten and accuse. Even when the facts took our breath away, we held them up triumphantly. Look at this!

I had enrolled in the seminar out of sheer curiosity. It was finally something new, not contracts and not property, torts or criminal law or legal method. I brought to the seminar my arrogant, superior airs. But as the winter went on, I found it harder and harder to withdraw—either from the events we read and heard about, or from the zeal that seized the students in the seminar. At first, I pretended to myself that I only wanted to participate in the scholarly debate, or its political and moral fervor. But I wanted more; I wanted to share in the general passion. The others may have found me distant and arrogant; for my part, I had the good feeling all that winter that I belonged, and that I was at peace with myself about what I was doing and the people with whom I was doing it.

CHAPTER THREE

*T*HE TRIAL was in another town, about an hour's drive away. I had no other reason ever to go there. Another student drove. He had grown up there and knew the place.

It was a Thursday. The trial had begun on Monday. The first three days of proceedings had been taken up with defense motions to recuse. Our group was the fourth, and so would witness the examination of the defendants at the actual start of proceedings.

We drove along Bergstrasse under blossoming fruit trees. We were bubbling over with exhilaration: finally we could put all our training into practice. We did not feel like mere spectators, or listeners, or recorders. Watching and listening and recording were our contributions to the exploration of history.

The court was in a turn-of-the-century building, but devoid of the gloomy pomposity so characteristic of court buildings of the time. The room that housed the assize court had a row of large windows down the left-hand side, with milky glass that blocked the view of the outdoors but let in a great deal of light. The prosecutors sat in front of the windows, and against the bright spring and summer daylight they were no more than black silhouettes. The court, three judges in black robes and six selected local citizens, was in place at the head of the courtroom and on the right-hand side was the bench of defendants and their lawyers: there were so many of them that the extra chairs and tables stretched into the middle of the room in front of the public seats. Some of the defendants and their lawyers were sitting with their backs to us. One of them was Hanna. I did not recognize her until she was called, and she stood up and stepped forward. Of course I recognized the name as soon as I heard it: Hanna Schmitz. Then I also recognized the body, the head with the hair gathered in an unfamiliar knot, the neck, the broad back, and the strong arms. She held herself very straight, balanced on both feet. Her arms were relaxed at her sides. She wore a gray dress with short sleeves. I recognized her, but I felt nothing. Nothing at all.

Yes, she wished to stand. Yes, she was born on October 21, 1922, near Hermannstadt and was now forty-three years old. Yes, she had worked at

Siemens in Berlin and had joined the SS in the autumn of 1943.

"You enrolled voluntarily?

"Yes."

"Why?"

Hanna did not answer.

"Is it true that you joined the SS even though Siemens had offered you a job as a foreman?"

Hanna's lawyer was on his feet. "What do you mean by 'even though'? Do you mean to suggest that a woman should prefer to become a foreman at Siemens than join the SS? There are no grounds for making my client's decision the object of such a question."

He sat down. He was the only young defense attorney; the others were old—some of them, as became apparent, old Nazis. Hanna's lawyer avoided both their jargon and their lines of reasoning. But he was too hasty and too zealous in ways that were as damaging to his client as his colleagues' Nazi tirades were to theirs. He did succeed in making the judge look irritated and stop pursuing the question of why Hanna had joined the SS. But the impression remained that she had done it of her own accord and not under pressure. It didn't help her when one of the legal members of the court asked Hanna what kind of work she expected to do for the SS and she said that the SS was recruiting women at Siemens and other factories for guard duties and she had applied and was hired.

To the judge's questions, Hanna testified in monosyllables that yes, she had served in Auschwitz until early 1944 and then in a small camp near Cracow until the winter of 1944–45, that yes, when the prisoners were moved to the west she went with them all the way, that she was in Kassel at the end of the war and since then had lived in one place and another. She had been in my city for eight years; it was the longest time she had spent in any one place.

"Is her frequent change of residence supposed to be grounds for viewing her as a flight risk?" The lawyer was openly sarcastic. "My client registered with the police each time she arrived at a new address and each time she left. There is no reason to assume she would run away, and there is nothing for her to hide. Did the judge feel it impossible to release my client on her own recognizance because of the gravity of the charges and the risk of public agitation? That, members of the court, is a Nazi rationale for custody; it was introduced by the Nazis and abolished after the Nazis. It no longer exists." The lawyer's malicious emphasis underlined the irony in this truth.

I was jolted. I realized that I had assumed it was both natural and right that Hanna should be in custody. Not because of the charges, the gravity of the allegations, or the force of the evidence, of which I had no real knowledge yet, but because in a cell she was out of my world, out of my life. I wanted her far away from me, so unattainable that she could con-

tinue as the mere memory she had become and remained all these years. If the lawyer was successful, I
would have to prepare myself to meet her again, and
I would have to work out how I wanted to do that,
and how it should be. And I could see no reason why
he should fail. If Hanna had not tried to escape the
law so far, why should she try now? And what evidence could she suppress? There were no other legal
reasons at that time to hold someone in custody.

The judge seemed irritated again, and I began to
realize that this was his particular trick. Whenever he
found a statement either obstructionist or annoying,
he took off his glasses, stared at the speaker with a
blank, short-sighted gaze, frowned, and either ignored the statement altogether or began with "So you
mean" or "So what you're trying to say is" and then
repeated what had been said in a way as to leave no
doubt that he had no desire to deal with it and that
trying to compel him to do so would be pointless.

"So you're saying that the arresting judge misin-
terpreted the fact that the defendant ignored all letters and summonses, and did not present herself
either to the police, or the prosecutor, or the judge?
You wish to make a motion to lift the order of de-
tention?"

The lawyer made the motion and the court denied it.

CHAPTER FOUR

I DID NOT miss a single day of the trial. The other students were surprised. The professor was pleased that one of us was making sure that the next group learned what the last one had heard and seen.

Only once did Hanna look at the spectators and over at me. Usually she was brought in by a guard and took her place and then kept her eyes fixed on the bench throughout the day's proceedings. It appeared arrogant, as did the fact that she didn't talk to the other defendants and almost never with her lawyer either. However, as the trial went on, the other defendants talked less among themselves too. When there were breaks in the proceedings, they stood with relatives and friends, and in the mornings they waved and called hello to them when they saw them in the public benches. During the breaks Hanna remained in her seat.

So I watched her from behind. I saw her head, her neck, her shoulders. I decoded her head, her neck, her shoulders. When she was being discussed, she held her head very erect. When she felt she was being unjustly treated, slandered, or attacked and she was struggling to respond, she rolled her shoulders forward and her neck swelled, showing the play of muscles. The objections were regularly overruled, and her shoulders regularly sank. She never shrugged, and she never shook her head. She was too keyed up to allow herself anything as casual as a shrug or a shake of the head. Nor did she allow herself to hold her head at an angle, or to let it fall, or to lean her chin on her hand. She sat as if frozen. It must have hurt to sit that way.

Sometimes strands of hair slipped out of the tight knot, began to curl, lay on the back of her neck, and moved gently against it in the draft. Sometimes Hanna wore a dress with a neckline low enough to reveal the birthmark high on her left shoulder. Then I remembered how I had blown the hair away from that neck and how I had kissed that birthmark and that neck. But the memory was like a retrieved file. I felt nothing.

During the weeks of the trial, I felt nothing: my feelings were numbed. Sometimes I poked at them, and imagined Hanna doing what she was accused of doing as clearly as I could, and also doing what the hair on her neck and the birthmark on her shoulder recalled to my mind. It was like a hand pinching an arm numbed by an injection. The arm doesn't register that it is being pinched by the hand, the hand registers that it is pinching the arm, and at first the mind cannot tell the two of them apart. But a moment later it distinguishes them quite clearly. Perhaps the hand has pinched so hard that the flesh stays white for a while. Then the blood flows back and the spot regains its color. But that does not bring back sensation.

Who had given me the injection? Had I done it myself, because I couldn't manage without anesthesia? The anesthetic functioned not only in the courtroom, and not only to allow me to see Hanna as if it was someone else who had loved and desired her, someone I knew well but who wasn't me. In every part of my life, too, I stood outside myself and watched; I saw myself functioning at the university, with my parents and brother and sister and my friends, but inwardly I felt no involvement.

After a time I thought I could detect a similar numbness in other people. Not in the lawyers, who carried on throughout the trial with the same rhetorical legalistic pugnacity, jabbing pedantry, or loud, calculated truculence, depending on their personalities and their political standpoint. Admittedly the trial proceedings exhausted them; in the evenings they were tired and got more shrill. But overnight they recharged or reinflated themselves and droned and hissed away the next morning just as they had twenty-four hours before. The prosecutors made an effort to keep up and display the same level of attack day after day. But they didn't succeed, at first because the facts and their outcome as laid out at the trial horrified them so much, and later because the numbness began to take hold. The effect was strongest on the judges and the lay members of the court. During the first weeks of the trial they took in the horrors—sometimes recounted in tears, sometimes in choking voices, sometimes in agitated or broken sentences—with visible shock or obvious efforts at self-control. Later their faces returned to normal; they could smile and whisper to one another or even show traces of impatience when a witness lost the thread while testifying. When going to Israel to question a witness was discussed, they started getting the travel bug. The other students kept being horrified all over again. They only came to the trial once a week, and each time the same thing happened: the intrusion of horror into daily life. I, who was in court every day, observed their reactions with detachment.

It was like being a prisoner in the death camps who survives month after month and becomes accustomed to the life, while he registers with an objective eye the horror of the new arrivals: registers it with the same numbness that he brings to the murders and deaths themselves. All survivor literature talks about this numbness, in which life's functions are reduced to a minimum, behavior becomes completely selfish and indifferent to others, and gassing and burning are everyday occurrences. In the rare accounts by perpetrators, too, the gas chambers and ovens become ordinary scenery, the perpetrators reduced to their few functions and exhibiting a mental paralysis and indifference, a dullness that makes them seem drugged or drunk. The defendants seemed to me to be trapped still, and forever, in this drugged state, in a sense petrified in it.

Even then, when I was preoccupied by this general numbness, and by the fact that it had taken hold not only of the perpetrators and victims, but of all of us, judges and lay members of the court, prosecutors and recorders, who had to deal with these events now; when I likened perpetrators, victims, the dead, the living, survivors, and their descendants to each other, I didn't feel good about it and I still don't.

Can one see them all as linked in this way? When I began to make such comparisons in discussions, I always emphasized that the linkage was not meant to relativize the difference between being forced into the world of the death camps and entering it voluntarily, between enduring suffering and imposing it on others, and that this difference was of the greatest, most critical importance. But I met with shock and indignation when I said this not in reaction to the others' objections, but before they had even had the chance to demur.

At the same time I ask myself, as I had already begun to ask myself back then: What should our second generation have done, what should it do with the knowledge of the horrors of the extermination of the Jews? We should not believe we can comprehend the incomprehensible, we may not compare the incomparable, we may not inquire because to inquire is to make the horrors an object of discussion, even if the horrors themselves are not questioned, instead of accepting them as something in the face of which we can only fall silent in revulsion, shame, and guilt. Should we only fall silent in revulsion, shame, and guilt? To what purpose? It was not that I had lost my eagerness to explore and cast light on things which had filled the seminar, once the trial got under way. But that some few would be convicted and punished while we of the second generation were silenced by revulsion, shame, and guilt—was that all there was to it now?

CHAPTER FIVE

    N THE SECOND week, the indictment was read out. It took a day and a half to read— a day and a half in the subjunctive. The first defendant is alleged to have . . . Furthermore she is alleged . . . In addition, she is alleged . . . Thus she comes under the necessary conditions of paragraph so-and-so, furthermore she is alleged to have committed this and that act . . . She is alleged to have acted illegally and culpably. Hanna was the fourth defendant.

The five accused women had been guards in a small camp near Cracow, a satellite camp for Auschwitz. They had been transferred there from Auschwitz in early 1944 to replace guards killed or injured in an explosion in the factory where the women in the camp worked. One count of the indictment involved their conduct at Auschwitz, but that was of minor significance compared with the other charges. I no longer remember it. Was it because it didn't involve Hanna, but only the other women? Was it of minor importance in relation to the other counts, or minor, period? Did it simply seem inexcusable to have someone available for trial who had been in Auschwitz and not charge them about their conduct in Auschwitz?

Of course the five defendants had not been in charge of the camp. There was a commandant, plus special troops, and other female guards. Most of the troops and guards had not survived the bombing raid that put an end one night to the prisoners' westward march. Some fled the same night, and vanished as surely as the commandant, who had made himself scarce as soon as the column of prisoners set off on the forced march to the west.

None of the prisoners should, by rights, have survived the night of the bombing. But two did survive, a mother and her daughter, and the daughter had written a book about the camp and the march west and published it in America. The police and prosecutors had tracked down not only the five defendants but several witnesses who had lived in the village which had taken the bombing hits that ended the death march. The most important witnesses were the daughter, who had come to Germany, and the mother, who had remained in Israel. To depose the mother the court, prosecutors, and defense

lawyers were going to go to Israel—the only part of
the trial I did not attend.

One main charge concerned selections in the
camp. Each month around sixty new women were
sent out from Auschwitz and the same number were
sent back, minus those who had died in the mean-
time. It was clear to everyone that the women would
be killed in Auschwitz; it was those who could no
longer perform useful work in the factory who were
sent back. The factory made munitions; the actual
work was not difficult, but the women hardly ever
got to do the actual work, because they had to do
raw construction to repair the devastating damage
caused by the explosion early in the year.

The other main charge involved the night of the
bombing that ended everything. The troops and
guards had locked the prisoners, several hundred
women, in a church in a village that had been abandoned by most of its inhabitants. Only a few bombs
fell, possibly intended for the nearby railroad or a factory, or maybe simply released because they were left
over from a raid on a larger town. One of them hit the
priest's house in which the troops and guards were
sleeping. Another landed on the church steeple. First
the steeple burned, then the roof; then the blazing
rafters collapsed into the nave, and the pews caught
fire. The heavy doors were unbudgeable. The defendants could have unlocked them. They did not, and
the women locked in the church burned to death.

CHAPTER SIX

*T*HE TRIAL could not have gone any worse for Hanna. She had already made a bad impression on the court during the preliminary questioning. After the indictment had been read out, she spoke up to say that something was incorrect; the presiding judge rebuked her irritably, telling her that she had had plenty of time before the trial to study the charges and register objections; now the trial was in progress and the evidence would show what was correct and incorrect. When the presiding judge proposed at the beginning of the actual testimony that the German version of the daughter's book not be read into the record, as it had been prepared for publication by a German publisher and the manuscript made available to all participants in the trial, Hanna had to be argued into it by her lawyer under the exasperated eyes of the judge. She did not willingly agree. She also did not want to acknowledge that she had admitted, in an earlier deposition, to having had the key to the church. She had not had the key, no one had had the key, there had not been any one key to the church, but several keys to several different doors, and they had all been left outside in the locks. But the court record of her examination by the judge, approved and signed by her, read differently, and the fact that she asked why they were trying to hang something on her did not make matters any better. She didn't ask loudly or arrogantly, but with determination, and, I think, in visible and audible confusion and helplessness, and the fact that she spoke of others trying to hang something on her did not mean she was claiming any miscarriage of justice by the court. But the presiding judge interpreted it that way and responded sharply. Hanna's lawyer leapt to his feet and let loose, overeagerly; he was asked whether he was agreeing with his client's accusations, and sat down again.

Hanna wanted to do the right thing. When she thought she was being done an injustice, she contradicted it, and when something was rightly claimed or alleged, she acknowledged it. She contradicted vigorously and admitted willingly, as though her admissions gave her the right to her contradictions or as though, along with her contradictions, she took on a responsibility to admit what she could not deny. But she did not notice that her insistence annoyed the presiding judge. She had no sense of context, of the rules of the game, of the formulas by which her statements and those of the others were toted up into guilt and innocence, conviction and acquittal. To compensate for her defective grasp of the situation, her lawyer would have had to have more experience and self-confidence, or simply to have been better. But Hanna should not have made things so hard for him; she was obviously withholding her trust from him, but had not chosen another lawyer she trusted more. Her lawyer was a public defender appointed by the court.

Sometimes Hanna achieved her own kind of success. I remember her examination on the selections in the camp. The other defendants denied ever having had anything to do with them. Hanna admitted so readily that she had participated—not alone, but just like the others and along with them—that the judge felt he had to probe further.

"What happened at the selections?"

Hanna described how the guards had agreed among themselves to tally the same number of prisoners from their six equal areas of responsibility, ten each and sixty in all, but that the figures could fluctuate when the number of sick was low in one person's area of responsibility and high in another's, and that all the guards on duty had decided together who was to be sent back.

"None of you held back, you all acted together?"

"Yes."

"Did you not know that you were sending the prisoners to their death?"

"Yes, but the new ones came, and the old ones had to make room for the new ones."

"So because you wanted to make room, you said you and you and you have to be sent back to be killed?"

Hanna didn't understand what the presiding judge was getting at.

"I . . . I mean . . . so what would you have done?" Hanna meant it as a serious question. She did not know what she should or could have done differently, and therefore wanted to hear from the judge, who seemed to know everything, what he would have done.

Everything was quiet for a moment. It is not the custom at German trials for defendants to question the judge. But now the question had been asked, and everyone was waiting for the judge's answer. He had to answer; he could not ignore the question or brush it away with a reprimand or a dismissive counterquestion. It was clear to everyone, it was clear to him too, and I understood why he had adopted an expression of irritation as his defining feature. It was his mask. Behind it, he could take a little time to find an answer. But not too long; the longer he took, the greater the tension and expectation, and the better his answer had to be.

"There are matters one simply cannot get drawn into, that one must distance oneself from, if the price is not life and limb."

Perhaps this would have been all right if he had said the same thing, but referred directly to Hanna or himself. Talking about what "one" must and must not do and what it costs did not do justice to the seriousness of Hanna's question. She had wanted to know what she should have done in her particular situation, not that there are things that are not done. The judge's answer came across as hapless and pathetic. Everyone felt it. They reacted with sighs of disappointment and stared in amazement at Hanna, who had more or less won the exchange. But she herself was lost in thought.

"So should I have . . . should I have not . . . should I not have signed up at Siemens?"

It was not a question directed at the judge. She was talking out loud to herself, hesitantly, because she had not yet asked herself that question and did not know whether it was the right one, or what the answer was.

ＪＵＳＴ ＡＳ Hanna's insistent contradictions annoyed the judge, her willingness to admit things annoyed the other defendants. It was damaging for their defense, but also her own.

In fact the evidence itself was favorable to the defendants. The only evidence for the main count of the indictment was the testimony of the mother who had survived, her daughter, and the daughter's book. A competent defense would have been able, without attacking the substance of the mother's and daughter's testimony, to cast reasonable doubt on whether these defendants were the actual ones who had done the selections. Witnesses' testimony on this point was not precise, nor could it be; there had, after all, been a commandant, uniformed men, other female guards, and a whole hierarchy of responsibilities and order with which the prisoners had only been partially confronted and which, correspondingly, they could only partially understand. The same was true of the second count. Mother and daughter had both been locked inside the church, and could not testify as to what had happened outside. Certainly the defendants could not claim not to have been there. The other witnesses who had been living in the village then had spoken with them and remembered them. But these other witnesses had to be careful to avoid the charge that they themselves could have rescued the prisoners. If the defendants had been the only ones there—could the villagers not have overpowered the few women and unlocked the church doors themselves? Would they not have to fall in line with the defense, that the defendants had acted under a power of compulsion that also extended to them, the witnesses? That they had been forced by, or acted on the orders of, the troops who had either not yet fled or who, in the reasonable assumption of the guards, had left for a brief interval, perhaps to bring the wounded to the field hospital, and would be returning soon?

When the other defendants' lawyers realized that such strategies were being undone by Hanna's voluntary concessions, they switched to another, which used her concessions to incriminate Hanna and exonerate the other defendants. The defense lawyers did this with professional objectivity. The other defendants backed them up with impassioned interjections.

"You stated that you knew you were sending the prisoners to their deaths—that was only true of you, wasn't it? You cannot know what your colleagues knew. Perhaps you can guess at it, but in the final analysis you cannot judge, is that not so?" Hanna was asked by one of the other defendants' lawyers.

"But we all knew . . ."

"Saying 'we,' 'we all' is easier than saying 'I,' 'I alone,' isn't it? Isn't it true that you and only you had special prisoners in the camp, young girls, first one for a period, and then another one?"

Hanna hesitated. "I don't think I was the only one who . . ."

"You dirty liar! Your favorites—all that was just you, no one else!" Another of the accused, a coarse woman, not unlike a fat broody hen but with a spiteful tongue, was visibly worked up.

"Is it possible that when you say 'knew,' the most you can actually do is assume, and that when you say 'believe,' you are actually just making things up?" The lawyer shook his head, as if disturbed by her acknowledgment of this. "And is it also true that once you were tired of your special prisoners, they all went back to Auschwitz with the next transport?"

Hanna did not answer.

"That was your special, your personal selection, wasn't it? You don't want to remember, you want to hide behind something that everyone did, but . . ."

"Oh God!" The daughter, who had taken a seat in the public benches after being examined, covered her face with her hands. "How could I have forgotten?" The presiding judge asked if she wished to add anything to her testimony. She did not wait to be called to the front. She stood up and spoke from her seat among the spectators.

"Yes, she had favorites, always one of the young ones who was weak and delicate, and she took them under her wing and made sure that they didn't have to work, got them better barracks space and took care of them and fed them better, and in the evenings she had them brought to her. And the girls were never allowed to say what she did with them in the evening, and we assumed she was . . . also because they all ended up on the transports, as if she had had her fun with them and then had got bored. But it wasn't like that at all, and one day one of them finally talked, and we learned that the girls read aloud to her, evening after evening after evening. That was better than if they . . . and better than working themselves to death on the building site. I must have thought it was better, or I couldn't have forgotten it. But was it better?" She sat down.

Hanna turned around and looked at me. Her eyes found me at once, and I realized that she had known the whole time I was there. She just looked at me. Her face didn't ask for anything, beg for anything, assure me of anything or promise anything. It simply presented itself. I saw how tense and exhausted she was. She had circles under her eyes, and on each cheek a line that ran from top to bottom that I'd never seen before, that weren't yet deep, but already marked her like scars. When I turned red under her gaze, she turned away and back to the judges' bench.

The presiding judge asked the lawyer who had cross-examined Hanna if he had any further questions for the defendant. He also asked Hanna's lawyer. Ask her, I thought. Ask her if she chose the weak and delicate girls, because they could never have stood up to the work on the building site anyway, because they would have been sent on the next transport to Auschwitz in any case, and because she wanted to make that final month bearable. Say it, Hanna. Say you wanted to make their last month bearable. That that was the reason for choosing the delicate and the weak. That there was no other reason, and could not be.

But the lawyer did not ask Hanna, and she did not speak of her own accord.

HE GERMAN version of the book that the daughter had written about her time in the camps did not appear until after the trial. During the trial the manuscript was available, but to those directly involved. I had to read the book in English, an unfamiliar and laborious exercise at the time. And as always, the alien language, unmastered and struggled over, created a strange concatenation of distance and immediacy. I worked through the book with particular thoroughness and yet did not make it my own. It remained as alien as the language itself.

Years later I reread it and discovered that it is the book that creates distance. It does not invite one to identify with it and makes no one sympathetic, neither the mother nor the daughter, nor those who shared their fate in various camps and finally in

Auschwitz and the satellite camp near Cracow. It never gives the barracks leaders, the female guards, or the uniformed security force clear enough faces or shapes for the reader to be able to relate to them, to judge their acts for better or worse. It exudes the very numbness I have tried to describe before. But even in her numbness the daughter did not lose the ability to observe and analyze. And she had not allowed herself to be corrupted either by self-pity or by the self-confidence she had obviously drawn from the fact that she had survived and not only come through the years in the camps but given literary form to them. She writes about herself and her pubescent, precocious, and, when necessary, cunning behavior with the same sobriety she uses to describe everything else.

Hanna is neither named in the book, nor is she recognizable or identifiable in any way. Sometimes I thought I recognized her in one of the guards, who was described as young, pretty, and conscientiously unscrupulous in the fulfillment of her duties, but I wasn't sure. When I considered the other defendants, only Hanna could be the guard described. But there had been other guards. In one camp the daughter had known a guard who was called "Mare," also young, beautiful, and diligent, but cruel and uncontrolled. The guard in the camp reminded her of that one. Had others drawn the same comparison? Did Hanna know about it? Did she remember it? Was that why she was upset when I compared her to a horse?

The camp near Cracow was the last stop for mother and daughter after Auschwitz. It was a step forward; the work was hard, but easier, the food was better, and it was better to sleep six women to a room than a hundred to a barracks. And it was warmer; the women could forage for wood on the way from the factory to the camp, and bring it back with them. There was the fear of selections, but it wasn't as bad as at Auschwitz. Sixty women were sent back each month, sixty out of around twelve hundred; that meant each prisoner had a life expectancy of twenty months, even if she only possessed average strength, and there was always the hope of being stronger than the average. Moreover, there was also the hope that the war would be over in less than twenty months.

The misery began when the camp was closed and the prisoners set off towards the west. It was winter, it was snowing, and the clothing in which the women had frozen in the factory and just managed to hold out in the camp was completely inadequate, but not as inadequate as what was on their feet, often rags and sheets of newspaper tied so as to stay on when they stood or walked around, but impossible to make withstand long marches in snow and ice. And the women did not just march; they were driven, and forced to run. "Death march?" asks the daughter in the book, and answers, "No, death trot, death gallop." Many collapsed along the way; others never got to their feet again after nights spent in barns or leaning against a wall. After a week, almost half the women were dead.

The church made a better shelter than the barns and walls the women had had before. When they had passed abandoned farms and stayed overnight, the uniformed security force and the female guards had taken the living quarters for themselves. Here, in the almost deserted village, they could commandeer the priest's house and still leave the prisoners something more than a barn or a wall. That they did it, and that the prisoners even got something warm to eat in the village seemed to promise an end to the misery. The women went to sleep. Shortly afterwards the bombs fell. As long as the steeple was the only thing burning, the fire could be heard in the church, but not seen. When the tip of the steeple collapsed and crashed down onto the rafters, it took several minutes for the glow of the fire to become visible. By then the flames were already licking downwards and setting clothes alight, collapsing burning beams set fire to the pews and pulpit, and soon the whole roof crashed into the nave and started a general conflagration.

The daughter thinks the women could have saved themselves if they had immediately gotten together to break down one of the doors. But by the time they

realized what had happened and was going to happen, and that no one was coming to open the doors,
it was too late. It was completely dark when the
sound of the falling bombs woke them. For a while
they heard nothing but an eerie, frightening noise
in the steeple, and kept absolutely quiet, so as to hear
the noise better and figure out what it was. That it
was the crackling and snapping of a fire, that it was
the glow of flames that flared up now and again behind the windows, that the crash above their heads
signaled the spreading of the fire from the steeple to
the roof—all this the women realized only once the
rafters began to burn. They realized, they screamed
in horror, screamed for help, threw themselves at the
doors, shook them, beat at them, screamed.

When the burning roof crashed into the nave, the
shell of the walls acted like a chimney. Most of the
women did not suffocate, but burned to death in
the brilliant roar of the flames. In the end, the fire
even burned its glowing way through the ironclad
church doors. But that was hours later.

Mother and daughter survived because the
mother did the right thing for the wrong reasons.
When the women began to panic, she couldn't bear
to be among them anymore. She fled to the gallery.
She didn't care that she was closer to the flames, she
just wanted to be alone, away from the screaming,
thrashing, burning women. The gallery was narrow,
so narrow that it was barely touched by the burning

beams. Mother and daughter stood pressed against the wall and saw and heard the raging of the fire. Next day they didn't dare come down and out of the church. In the darkness of the following night, they were afraid of not finding the stairs and the way out. When they left the church in the dawn of the day after that, they met some of the villagers, who gaped at them in silent astonishment, but gave them clothing and food and let them walk on.

CHAPTER NINE

"*W*HY DID you not unlock the doors?"
The presiding judge put the question to
one defendant after another. One after the other,
they gave the same answer. They couldn't unlock the
doors. Why? They had been wounded when the
bombs hit the priest's house. Or they had been in
shock as a result of the bombardment. Or they had
been busy after the bombs hit, with the wounded
guard contingent, pulling them out of the rubble,
bandaging them, taking care of them. They had not
thought about the church, had not seen the fire in
the church, had not heard the screams from the
church.

The judge made the same statement to one defendant after another. The record indicated otherwise.
This was deliberately phrased with caution. To say

that the record found in the SS archives said otherwise would be wrong. But it was true that it suggested something different. It listed the names of
those who had been killed in the priest's house and
those who had been wounded, those who had
brought the wounded to a field hospital in a truck,
and those who had accompanied the truck in a jeep.
It indicated that the women guards had stayed behind to wait out the end of the fires, to prevent any of
them from spreading and to prevent any attempts to
escape under the cover of the flames. It referred to
the death of the prisoners.

The fact that the names of the defendants appeared nowhere in the report suggested that the defendants were among the female guards who had
remained behind. That these guards had remained
behind to prevent attempts at escape indicated that
the affair didn't end with the rescue of the wounded
from the priest's house and the departure of the
transport to the field hospital. The guards who remained behind, the report indicated, had allowed
the fire to rage in the church and had kept the
church doors locked. Among the guards who remained behind, the report indicated, were the defendants.

No, said one defendant after the other, that is not
the way it was. The report was wrong. That much
was evident from the fact that it mentioned the obli-
gation of the guards to prevent the fires from spread-

ing. How could they have carried out that responsibility? It was ridiculous, as was the other responsibility of preventing attempted escapes under the cover of the fires. Attempted escapes? By the time they no longer had to worry about their own people and could worry about the others, the prisoners, there was no one left to escape. No, the report completely ignored what they had done and achieved and suffered that night. How could such a false report have been filed? They didn't know.

Until it was the turn of the plump and vicious defendant. She knew. "Ask that one there!" She pointed at Hanna. "She wrote the report. She's the guilty one, she did it all, and she wanted to use the report to cover it up and drag us into it."

The judge asked Hanna. But it was his last question. His first was "Why did you not unlock the doors?"

"We were . . . we had . . ." Hanna was groping for the answer. "We didn't have any alternative."

"You had no alternative?"

"Some of us were dead, and the others had left. They said they were taking the wounded to the field hospital and would come back, but they knew they weren't coming back, and so did we. Perhaps they didn't even go to the hospital, the wounded were not that badly hurt. We would have gone with them, but they said they needed the room for the wounded, and anyway they didn't . . . they weren't keen to have so many women along. I don't know where they went."

"What did you do?"

"We didn't know what to do. It all happened so fast, with the priest's house burning and the church spire, and the men and the cart were there one minute and gone the next, and suddenly we were alone with the women in the church. They left behind some weapons, but we didn't know how to use them, and even if we had, what good would it have done, since we were only a handful of women? How could we have guarded all those women? A line like that is very long, even if you keep it as tight together as possible, and to guard such a long column, you need far more people than we had." Hanna paused. "Then the screaming began and got worse and worse. If we had opened the doors and they had all come rushing out . . ."

The judge waited a moment. "Were you afraid? Were you afraid the prisoners would overpower you?"

"That they would . . . no, but how could we have restored order? There would have been chaos, and we had no way to handle that. And if they'd tried to escape . . ."

Once again the judge waited, but Hanna didn't finish the sentence. "Were you afraid that if they escaped, you would be arrested, convicted, shot?"

"We couldn't just let them escape! We were responsible for them . . . I mean, we had guarded them the whole time, in the camp and on the march, that was the point, that we had to guard them and not let them escape. That's why we didn't know what to do. We also had no idea how many of the women would survive the next few days. So many had died already, and the ones who were still alive were so weak . . ."

Hanna realized that what she was saying wasn't doing her case any good. But she couldn't say anything else. She could only try to say what she was saying better, to describe it better and explain it. But the more she said, the worse it looked for her. Because she was at her wit's end, she turned to the judge again.

"What would you have done?"

But this time she knew she would get no answer. She wasn't expecting one. Nobody was. The judge shook his head silently.

Not that it was impossible to imagine the confusion and helplessness Hanna described. The night, the cold, the snow, the fire, the screaming of the women in the church, the sudden departure of the people who had commanded and escorted the female guards—how could the situation have been easy? But could an acknowledgment that the situation had been hard be any mitigation for what the defendants had done or not done? As if it had been a car accident on a lonely road on a cold winter night, with injuries and totaled vehicles, and no one know-

ing what to do? Or as if it had been a conflict between two equally compelling duties that required
action? That is how one could imagine what Hanna
was describing, but nobody was willing to look at it
in such terms.

"Did you write the report?"

"We all discussed what we should write. We
didn't want to hang any of the blame on the ones
who had left. But we didn't want to attract charges
that we had done anything wrong either."

"So you're saying you talked it through together.
Who wrote it?"

"You!" The other defendant pointed at Hanna.

"No, I didn't write it. Does it matter who did?"

A prosecutor suggested that an expert be called to
compare the handwriting in the report and the
handwriting of the defendant Schmitz.

"My handwriting? You want my handwriting? . . ."

The judge, the prosecutor, and Hanna's lawyer
discussed whether a person's handwriting retains its
character over more than fifteen years and can be
identified. Hanna listened and tried several times to
say or ask something, and was becoming increas-
ingly alarmed. Then she said, "You don't have to call
an expert. I admit I wrote the report."

CHAPTER TEN

I HAVE NO memory of the Friday seminar meetings. Even when I recall the trial, I cannot remember what topics we selected for scholarly discussion. What did we talk about? What did we want to know? What did the professor teach us?

But I remember the Sundays. The days in court gave me a new hunger for the colors and smells of nature. On Fridays and Saturdays I managed to catch up on what I had missed of my studies during the other days of the week, so that I could complete my course assignments and pass the semester. On Sundays, I took off by myself.

Heiligenberg, St. Michael's Basilica, the Bismarck Tower, the Philosophers' Path, the banks of the river—I didn't vary my route much from one Sunday to the next. I found there was enough variety in the greens that became richer and richer from week to week, and in the floodplain of the Rhine, that was sometimes in a heat haze, sometimes hidden behind curtains of rain and sometimes overhung by storm clouds, and in the smells of the berries and wildflowers in the woods when the sun blazed down on them, and of earth and last year's rotting leaves when it rained. Anyway I don't need or seek much variety. Each journey a little further than the last, the next vacation in the new place I discovered during my last vacation and liked . . . For a while I thought I should be more daring, and made myself go to Ceylon, Egypt, and Brazil, before I went back to making familiar regions more familiar. I see more in them.

I have rediscovered the place in the woods where Hanna's secret became clear to me. There is nothing special about it now, nor was there anything special then, no strangely shaped tree or cliff, no unusual view of the city and the plain, nothing that would invite startling associations. In thinking about Hanna, going round and round in the same tracks week after week, one thought had split off, taken another direction, and finally produced its own conclusion. When it did so, it was done—it could have been anywhere, or at least anywhere the familiarity of the surroundings and the scenery allowed what was truly surprising, what didn't come like a bolt from the blue, but had been growing inside myself, to be recognized and accepted. It happened on a path that climbed steeply up the mountain, crossed the road, passed a spring, and then wound under old, tall, dark trees and out into light underbrush.

Hanna could neither read nor write.

That was why she had had people read to her. That was why she had let me do all the writing and reading on our bicycle trip and why she had lost control that morning in the hotel when she found my note, realized I would assume she knew what it said, and was afraid she'd be exposed. That was why she had avoided being promoted by the streetcar company; as a conductor she could conceal her weakness, but it would have become obvious when she was being trained to become a driver. That was also why she had refused the promotion at Siemens and become a guard. That was why she had admitted to writing the report in order to escape a confrontation with an expert. Had she talked herself into a corner at the trial for the same reason? Because she couldn't read the daughter's book or the indictment, couldn't see the openings that would allow her to build a defense, and thus could not prepare herself accordingly? Was that why she sent her chosen wards to Auschwitz? To silence them in case they had noticed something? And was that why she always chose the weak ones in the first place?

Was that why? I could understand that she was ashamed at not being able to read or write, and would rather drive me away than expose herself. I was no stranger to shame as the cause of behavior that was deviant or defensive, secretive or misleading or hurtful. But could Hanna's shame at being illiterate be sufficient reason for her behavior at the trial or in the camp? To accept exposure as a criminal for fear of being exposed as an illiterate? To commit crimes to avoid the same thing?

How often I have asked myself these same questions, both then and since. If Hanna's motive was fear of exposure—why opt for the horrible exposure as a criminal over the harmless exposure as an illiterate? Or did she believe she could escape exposure altogether? Was she simply stupid? And was she vain enough, and evil enough, to become a criminal simply to avoid exposure?

Both then and since, I have always rejected this. No, Hanna had not decided in favor of crime. She had decided against a promotion at Siemens, and fell into a job as a guard. And no, she had not dispatched the delicate and the weak on transports to Auschwitz because they had read to her; she had chosen them to read to her because she wanted to make their last month bearable before their inevitable dispatch to Auschwitz. And no, at the trial Hanna did not weigh exposure as an illiterate against exposure as a criminal. She did not calculate and she did not maneuver. She accepted that she would be called to account, and simply did not wish to endure further exposure. She was not pursuing her own interests, but fighting for her own truth, her own justice. Because she always had to dissimulate somewhat, and could never be completely candid, it was a pitiful truth and a pitiful justice, but it was hers, and the struggle for it was her struggle.

She must have been completely exhausted. Her struggle was not limited to the trial. She was struggling, as she always had struggled, not to show what she could do but to hide what she couldn't do. A life made up of advances that were actually frantic retreats and victories that were concealed defeats.

I was oddly moved by the discrepancy between what must have been Hanna's actual concerns when she left my hometown and what I had imagined and theorized at the time. I had been sure that I had driven her away because I had betrayed and denied her, when in fact she had simply been running away from being found out by the streetcar company. However, the fact that I had not driven her away did not change the fact that I had betrayed her. So I was still guilty. And if I was not guilty because one cannot be guilty of betraying a criminal, then I was guilty of having loved a criminal.

CHAPTER ELEVEN

*O*NCE HANNA admitted having written the report, the other defendants had an easy game to play. When Hanna had not been acting alone, they claimed, she had pressured, threatened, and forced the others. She had seized command. She did the talking and the writing. She had made the decisions.

The villagers who testified could neither confirm nor deny this. They had seen that the burning church was guarded by several women who did not unlock it, and they had not dared to unlock it themselves. They had met the women the next morning as they were leaving the village, and recognized them as the defendants. But which of the defendants had been the spokeswoman at the early-morning encounter, or if anyone had played the role of spokeswoman, they could not recall.

"But you cannot rule out that it was this defendant"—the lawyer for one of the other defendants pointed at Hanna—"who took the decisions?"

They couldn't, how could they even have wanted to, and faced with the other defendants, visibly older, more worn out, more cowardly and bitter, they had no such impulse. In comparison with the other defendants, Hanna was the dominant one. Besides, the existence of a leader exonerated the villagers; having failed to achieve rescue in the face of a fiercely led opposing force looked better than having failed to do anything when confronted by a group of confused women.

Hanna kept struggling. She admitted what was true and disputed what was not. Her arguments became more desperate and more vehement. She didn't raise her voice, but her very intensity alienated the court.

Eventually she gave up. She spoke only when asked a direct question; her answers were short, minimal, sometimes beside the point. As if to make clear that she had given up, she now remained seated when speaking. The presiding judge, who had told her several times at the beginning of the trial that she did not need to stand and could remain seated if she preferred, was put off by this as well. Towards the end of the trial, I sometimes had the sense that the court had had enough, that they wanted to get the whole thing over with, that they were no longer paying attention but were some-where else, or rather here—back in the present after long weeks in the past.

I had had enough too. But I couldn't put it behind me. For me, the proceedings were not ending, but just beginning. I had been a spectator, and then sud-denly a participant, a player, and member of the jury. I had neither sought nor chosen this new role, but it was mine whether I wanted it or not, whether I did anything or just remained completely passive.

"Did anything"—there was only one thing to do. I could go to the judge and tell him that Hanna was illiterate. That she was not the main protagonist and guilty party the way the others made her out to be. That her behavior at the trial was not proof of singu-lar incorrigibility, lack of remorse, or arrogance, but was born of her incapacity to familiarize herself with the indictment and the manuscript and also proba-bly of her consequent lack of any sense of strategy or tactics. That her defense had been significantly com-promised. That she was guilty, but not as guilty as it appeared.

Maybe I would not be able to convince the judge. But I would give him enough to have to think about and investigate further. In the end, it would be proved that I was right, and Hanna would be pun-ished, but less severely. She would have to go to prison, but would be released sooner—wasn't that what she had been fighting for?

Yes, that was what she had been fighting for, but she was not willing to earn victory at the price of exposure as an illiterate. Nor would she want me to barter her self-image for a few years in prison. She could have made that kind of trade herself, and did not, which meant she didn't want it. Her sense of self was worth more than the years in prison to her.

But was it really worth all that? What did she gain from this false self-image which ensnared her and crippled her and paralyzed her? With the energy she put into maintaining the lie, she could have learned to read and write long ago.

I tried to talk about the problem with friends. Imagine someone is racing intentionally towards his own destruction and you can save him—do you go ahead and save him? Imagine there's an operation, and the patient is a drug user and the drugs are incompatible with the anesthetic, but the patient is ashamed of being an addict and does not want to tell the anesthesiologist—do you talk to the anesthesiologist? Imagine a trial and a defendant who will be convicted if he doesn't admit to being left-handed—do you tell the judge what's going on? Imagine he's gay, and could not have committed the crime because he's gay, but is ashamed of being gay. It isn't a question of whether the defendant should be ashamed of being left-handed or gay—just imagine that he is.

CHAPTER TWELVE

$\mathscr{I}$ DECIDED TO speak to my father. Not because we were particularly close. My father was undemonstrative, and could neither share his feelings with us children nor deal with the feelings we had for him. For a long time I believed there must be a wealth of undiscovered treasure behind that uncommunicative manner, but later I wondered if there was anything behind it at all. Perhaps he had been full of emotions as a boy and a young man, and by giving them no outlet had allowed them over the years to wither and die.

But it was because of the distance between us that I sought him out now. I wanted to talk to the philosopher who had written about Kant and Hegel, and who had, as I knew, occupied himself with moral issues. He should be well positioned to explore my problem in the abstract and, unlike my friends, to avoid getting trapped in the inadequacies of my examples.

When we children wanted to speak to our father, he gave us appointments just like his students. He worked at home and only went to the university to give his lectures and seminars. Colleagues and students who wished to speak to him came to see him at home. I remember lines of students leaning against the wall in the corridor and waiting their turn, some reading, some looking at the views of cities hanging in the corridor, others staring into space, all of them silent except for an embarrassed greeting when we children went down the corridor and said hello. We ourselves didn't have to wait in the hall when our father had made an appointment with us. But we too had to be at his door at the appointed time and knock to be admitted.

I knew two of my father's studies. The windows in the first one, in which Hanna had run her fingers along the books, looked out onto the streets and houses. The windows in the second looked out over the plain along the Rhine. The house we moved to in the early 1960s, and where my parents stayed after we had grown up, was on the big hill above the city. In both places, the windows did not open the room to the world beyond, but framed and hung the world in it like a picture. My father's study was a capsule in which books, papers, thoughts, and pipe and cigar smoke had created their own force field, different from that of the outside world.

My father allowed me to present my problem in its abstract form and with my examples. "It has to do with the trial, doesn't it?" But he shook his head to show that he didn't expect an answer, or want to press me or hear anything that I wasn't ready to tell him of my own accord. Then he sat, head to one side, hands gripping the arms of his chair, and thought. He didn't look at me. I studied him, his gray hair, his face, carelessly shaven as always, the deep lines between his eyes and from his nostrils to the corners of his mouth. I waited.

When he answered, he went all the way back to beginnings. He instructed me about the individual, about freedom and dignity, about the human being as subject and the fact that one may not turn him into an object. "Don't you remember how furious you would get as a little boy when Mama knew better what was good for you? Even how far one can act like this with children is a real problem. It is a philosophical problem, but philosophy does not concern itself with children. It leaves them to pedagogy, where they're not in very good hands. Philosophy has forgotten about children." He smiled at me. "Forgotten them forever, not just sometimes, the way I forget about you."

"But . . ."

"But with adults I see absolutely no justification for setting other people's views of what is good for them above their own ideas of what is good for themselves."

"Not even if they themselves are happy about it later?"

He shook his head. "We're not talking about happiness, we're talking about dignity and freedom. Even as a little boy, you knew the difference. It was no comfort to you that your mother was always right."

Today I like thinking back on that conversation with my father. I had forgotten it until after his death, when I began to search the depths of my memory for happy encounters and shared activities and experiences with him. When I found it, I was both amazed and delighted. Originally I was confused by my father's mixing of abstraction and concreteness. But eventually I sorted out what he had said to mean that I did not have to speak to the judge, that indeed I had no right to speak to him, and was relieved.

My father saw my relief. "That's how you like your philosophy?"

"Well, I didn't know if one had to act in the circumstances I described, and I wasn't really happy with the idea that one must, and if one really isn't allowed to do anything at all, I find that . . ." I didn't know what to say. A relief? A comfort? Appealing? That didn't sound like morality and responsibility. "I think that's good" would have sounded moral and responsible, but I couldn't say I thought it was good, that I thought it was any more than a relief.

"Appealing?" my father suggested.

I nodded and shrugged my shoulders.

"No, your problem has no appealing solution. Of course one must act if the situation as you describe it is one of accrued or inherited responsibility. If one knows what is good for another person who in turn is blind to it, then one must try to open his eyes. One has to leave him the last word, but one must talk to him, to him and not to someone else behind his back."

Talk to Hanna? What would I say to her? That I had seen through her lifelong lie? That she was in the process of sacrificing her whole life to this silly lie? That the lie wasn't worth the sacrifice? That that was why she should fight not to remain in prison any longer than she had to, because there was so much she could still do with her life afterwards? Could I deprive her of her lifelong lie, without opening some vision of a future to her? I had no idea what that might be, nor did I know how to face her and say that after what she had done it was right that her short- and medium-term future would be prison. I didn't know how to face her and say anything at all. I didn't know how to face her.

I asked my father: "And what if you can't talk to him?"

He looked at me doubtfully, and I knew myself that the question was beside the point. There was nothing more to moralize about. I just had to make a decision.

"I haven't been able to help you." My father stood up and so did I. "No, you don't have to go, it's just that my back hurts." He stood bent over, with his hands pressed against his kidneys. "I can't say that I'm sorry I can't help you. As a philosopher, I mean, which is how you were addressing me. As your father, I find the experience of not being able to help my children almost unbearable."

I waited, but he didn't say anything else. I thought he was making it easy on himself; I knew when he could have taken care of us more and how he could have helped us more. Then I thought that perhaps he realized this himself and really found it difficult to bear. But either way I had nothing to say to him. I was embarrassed, and had the feeling he was embarrassed too.

"Well then . . ."

"You can come any time." My father looked at me.

I didn't believe him, and nodded.

CHAPTER THIRTEEN

*I*N JUNE, the court flew to Israel for two weeks. The hearing there took only a few days, but the judge and prosecutors made it a combined judicial and touristic outing, Jerusalem and Tel Aviv, the Negev and the Red Sea. It was undoubtedly all aboveboard as regards rules of conduct, vacations, and expense accounts, but I found it bizarre nonetheless.

I had planned to devote these two weeks to my studies. But it didn't go the way I had imagined and planned. I couldn't concentrate enough to learn anything, either from the professors or my books. Again and again, my thoughts wandered off and were lost in images.

I saw Hanna by the burning church, hard-faced, in a black uniform, with a riding whip. She drew circles in the snow with her whip, and slapped it against her boots. I saw her being read to. She listened carefully, asked no questions, and made no comments. When the hour was over, she told the reader she would be going on the transport to Auschwitz next morning. The reader, a frail creature with a stubble of black hair and nearsighted eyes, began to cry. Hanna hit the wall with her hand and two women, also prisoners in striped clothing, came in and pulled the reader away. I saw Hanna walking the paths in the camp, going into the prisoners' barracks and overseeing construction work. She did it all with the same hard face, cold eyes, and pursed mouth, and the prisoners ducked, bent over their work, pressed themselves against the wall, into the wall, wanted to disappear into the wall. Sometimes there were many prisoners gathered together or running from one place to the other or standing in line or marching, and Hanna stood among them and screamed orders, her screaming face a mask of ugliness, and helped things along with her whip. I saw the church steeple crashing into the roof and the sparks flying and heard the desperation of the women. I saw the burned-out church next morning.

Alongside these images, I saw the others. Hanna pulling on her stockings in the kitchen, standing by the bathtub holding the towel, riding her bicycle with skirts flying, standing in my father's study, dancing in front of the mirror, looking at me at the pool, Hanna listening to me, talking to me, laughing at me, loving me. Hanna loving me with cold eyes and pursed mouth, silently listening to me reading, and at the end banging the wall with her hand, talking to me with her face turning into a mask. The worst were the dreams in which a hard, imperious, cruel Hanna aroused me sexually; I woke from them full of longing and shame and rage. And full of fear about who I really was.

I knew that my fantasized images were poor clichés. They were unfair to the Hanna I had known and still knew. But still they were very powerful. They undermined my actual memories of Hanna and merged with the images of the camps that I had in my mind.

When I think today about those years, I realize how little direct observation there actually was, how few photographs that made life and murder in the camps real. We knew the gate of Auschwitz with its inscription, the stacked wooden bunks, the piles of hair and spectacles and suitcases; we knew the building that formed the entrance to Birkenau with the tower, the two wings, and the entryway for the trains, and from Bergen-Belsen the mountains of corpses found and photographed by the Allies at the liberation. We were familiar with some of the testimony of prisoners, but many of them were published soon after the war and not reissued until the 1980s, and in the intervening years they disappeared from publishers' lists. Today there are so many books and films that the world of the camps is part of our collective imagination and completes our ordinary everyday one. Our imagination knows its way around in it, and since the television series *Holocaust* and movies like *Sophie's Choice* and especially *Schindler's List,* actually moves in it, not just registering, but supplementing and embellishing it. Back then, the imagination was almost static: the shattering fact of the world of the camps seemed properly beyond its operations. The few images derived from Allied photographs and the testimony of survivors flashed on the mind again and again, until they froze into clichés.

CHAPTER FOURTEEN

I DECIDED TO go away. If I had been able to leave for Auschwitz the next day, I would have gone. But it would have taken weeks to get a visa. So I went to Struthof in Alsace. It was the nearest concentration camp. I had never seen one. I wanted reality to drive out the clichés.

I hitchhiked, and remember a ride in a truck with a driver who downed one bottle of beer after another, and a Mercedes driver who steered wearing white gloves. After Strasbourg I got lucky; the driver was going to Schirmeck, a small town not far from Struthof.

When I told the driver where I was going, he fell silent. I looked over at him, but couldn't tell why he had suddenly stopped talking in the midst of a lively conversation. He was middle-aged, with a haggard face and a dark red birthmark or scar on his right temple, and his black hair was carefully parted and combed in strands. He stared at the road in concentration.

The hills of the Vosges rolled out ahead of us. We were driving through vineyards into a wide-open valley that climbed gently. To the left and right, mixed forests grew up the slopes, and sometimes there was a quarry or a brick-walled factory with a corrugated iron roof, or an old sanatorium, or a large turreted villa among tall trees. A train track ran alongside us, sometimes to the left and sometimes to the right.

Then he spoke again. He asked me why I was visiting Struthof, and I told him about the trial and my lack of first-hand knowledge.

"Ah, you want to understand why people can do such terrible things." He sounded as if he was being a little ironic, but maybe it was just the tone of voice and the choice of words. Before I could reply, he went on: "What is it you want to understand? That people murder out of passion, or love, or hate, or for honor or revenge, that you understand?"

I nodded.

"You also understand that people murder for money or power? That people murder in wars and revolutions?"

I nodded again. "But . . ."

"But the people who were murdered in the camps hadn't done anything to the individuals who murdered them? Is that what you want to say? Do you mean that there was no reason for hatred, and no war?"

I didn't want to nod again. What he said was true, but not the way he said it.

"You're right, there was no war, and no reason for hatred. But executioners don't hate the people they execute, and they execute them all the same. Because they're ordered to? You think they do it because they're ordered to? And you think that I'm talking about orders and obedience, that the guards in the camps were under orders and had to obey?" He laughed sarcastically. "No, I'm not talking about orders and obedience. An executioner is not under orders. He's doing his work, he doesn't hate the people he executes, he's not taking revenge on them, he's not killing them because they're in his way or threatening him or attacking him. They're a matter of such indifference to him that he can kill them as easily as not."

He looked at me. "No 'buts'? Come on, tell me that one person cannot be that indifferent to another. Isn't that what they taught you? Solidarity with everything that has a human face? Human dignity? Reverence for life?"

I was outraged and helpless. I searched for a word, a sentence that would erase what he had said and strike him dumb.

"Once," he went on, "I saw a photograph of Jews being shot in Russia. The Jews were in a long row, naked; some were standing at the edge of a pit and behind them were soldiers with guns, shooting them in the neck. It was in a quarry, and above the Jews and the soldiers there was an officer sitting on a ledge in the rock, swinging his legs and smoking a cigarette. He looked a little morose. Maybe things weren't going fast enough for him. But there was also something satisfied, even cheerful about his expression, perhaps because the day's work was getting done and it was almost time to go home. He didn't hate the Jews. He wasn't . . ."

"Was it you? Were you sitting on the ledge and . . ."

He stopped the car. He was absolutely white, and the mark on his temple glistened. "Out!"

I got out. He swung the wheel so fast I had to jump aside. I still heard him as he took the next few curves. Then everything was silent.

I walked up the road. No car passed me, none came in the opposite direction. I heard birds, the wind in the trees, and the occasional murmur of a stream. In a quarter of an hour I reached the concentration camp.

CHAPTER FIFTEEN

I WENT BACK there not long ago. It was winter, a clear, cold day. Beyond Schirmeck the woods were snowy, the trees powdered white and the ground white too. The grounds of the concentration camp, an elongated area on a sloping terrace of mountain with a broad view of the Vosges, lay white in the bright sunshine. The gray-blue painted wood of the two- and three-story watchtowers and the one-story barracks made a pleasant contrast with the snow. True, there was the entryway festooned with barbed wire and the sign CONCENTRATION CAMP STRUTHOF-NATZWEILER and the double barbed-wire fence that surrounded the camp. But the ground between the remaining barracks, where more barracks had once stood side by side, no longer showed any trace of the camp under its glittering cover of snow. It could have been a sledding slope for children, spending their winter vacation in the cheerful barracks with the homely many-paned windows, and about to be called indoors for cake and hot chocolate.

The camp was closed. I tramped around it in the snow, getting my feet wet. I could easily see the whole grounds, and remembered how on my first visit I had gone down the steps that led between the foundations of the former barracks. I also remembered the ovens of the crematorium that were on display in another barracks, and that another barracks had contained cells. I remembered my vain attempts, back then, to imagine in concrete detail a camp filled with prisoners and guards and suffering. I really tried; I looked at a barracks, closed my eyes, and imagined row upon row of barracks. I measured a barracks, calculated its occupants from the informational booklet, and imagined how crowded it had been. I found out that the steps between the barracks had also been used for roll call, and as I looked from the bottom of the camp up towards the top, I filled them with rows of backs. But it was all in vain, and I had a feeling of the most dreadful, shameful failure.

On the way back, further down the hill, I found a small house opposite a restaurant that had a sign on it indicating that it had been a gas chamber. It was painted white, had doors and windows framed in sandstone, and could have been a barn or a shed or servants' living quarters. This building, too, was closed and I didn't remember if I had gone inside it on my first visit. I didn't get out of the car. I sat for a while with the motor running, and looked. Then I drove on.

At first I was embarrassed to meander home through the Alsatian villages looking for a restaurant where I could have lunch. But my awkwardness was not the result of real feeling, but of thinking about the way one is supposed to feel after visiting a concentration camp. I noticed this myself, shrugged, and found a restaurant called Au Petit Garçon in a village on a slope of the Vosges. My table looked out over the plain. Hanna had called me kid.

The previous time I had walked around the concentration camp grounds until they closed. Then I had sat down under the memorial that stood above the camp, and looked down over the grounds. I felt a great emptiness inside, as if I had been searching for some glimpse, not outside but within myself, and had discovered that there was nothing to be found.

Then it got dark. I had to wait an hour until the driver of a small open truck let me climb up and sit on the truck bed and took me to the next village, and I gave up the idea of hitchhiking back that same day. I found a cheap room in a guest house in the village and had a thin steak with french fries and peas in the dining room.

Four men were loudly playing cards at the next table. The door opened and a little old man came in without greeting anyone. He wore short pants and had a wooden leg. He ordered a beer at the bar. He sat facing away from the neighboring table, so that all they saw was his back and the back of his overly enlarged, bald skull. The card players laid down their cards, reached into the ashtrays, picked up the butts, took aim, and hit him. The man at the bar flapped his hands behind his head as if swatting away flies. The innkeeper set his beer in front of him. No one said a word.

I couldn't stand it. I jumped up and went over to the next table. "Stop it!" I was shaking with outrage. At that moment, the man half hobbled, half hopped over and began fumbling with his leg; suddenly he was holding the wooden leg in both hands. He brought it crashing down onto the table so that the glasses and ashtrays danced, and fell into an empty chair, laughing a squeaky, toothless laugh as the others laughed in a beery rumble along with him. "Stop it!" they laughed, pointing at me. "Stop it!"

During the night the wind howled around the house. I was not cold, and the noise of the wind and the creaking of the tree in front of the house and the occasional banging of a shutter were not enough to have kept me awake. But I became more and more inwardly restless, until my whole body began to shiver. I felt afraid, not in anticipation that something bad was going to happen, but in a physical way. I lay there, listening to the wind, feeling relieved every time it weakened and died down, but dreading its renewed assaults and not knowing how I would get out of bed next day, hitchhike back, continue my studies, and one day have a career and a wife and children.

I wanted simultaneously to understand Hanna's crime and to condemn it. But it was too terrible for that. When I tried to understand it, I had the feeling I was failing to condemn it as it must be condemned. When I condemned it as it must be condemned, there was no room for understanding. But even as I wanted to understand Hanna, failing to understand her meant betraying her all over again. I could not resolve this. I wanted to pose myself both tasks—understanding and condemnation. But it was impossible to do both.

The next day was another beautiful summer day. Hitchhiking was easy, and I got back in a few hours. I walked through the city as though I had been away for a long time; the streets and buildings and people looked strange to me. But that didn't mean the other world of the concentration camps felt any closer. My impressions of Struthof joined my few already existing images of Auschwitz and Bergen-Belsen, and froze along with them.

I DID GO to the presiding judge after all. I couldn't make myself visit Hanna. But neither could I endure doing nothing.

Why didn't I manage to speak to Hanna? She had left me, deceived me, was not the person I had taken her for or imagined her to be. And who had I been for her? The little reader she used, the little bedmate with whom she'd had her fun? Would she have sent me to the gas chamber if she hadn't been able to leave me, but wanted to get rid of me?

Why did I find it unendurable to do nothing? I told myself I had to prevent a miscarriage of justice. I had to make sure justice was done, despite Hanna's lifelong lie, justice both for and against Hanna, so to speak. But I wasn't really concerned with justice. I couldn't leave Hanna the way she was, or wanted to be. I had to meddle with her, have some kind of influence and effect on her, if not directly then indirectly.

The judge knew about our seminar group and was happy to invite me to come and talk after a session in court. I knocked, was invited in, greeted, and offered the chair in front of his desk. He was sitting in his shirtsleeves behind it. His robe hung over the back and arms of his chair; he had sat down in the robe and then slipped out of it. He seemed relaxed, a man who had finished his day's work and was content. Without the irritated expression he hid behind during the trial, he had a nice, intelligent, harmless civil servant's face.

He made general easy chitchat, asking me about this and that: what our seminar group thought of the trial, what our professor intended to do with the trial record, which semester we were in, which semester I was in, why I was studying law and when I planned to take my exams. He told me I must be sure to register for the exams on time.

I answered all his questions. Then I listened while he talked about his studies and his exams. He had done everything the right way. He had taken the right classes and seminars at the right time and had passed his final exams with the right degree of success. He liked being a lawyer and a judge, and if he had to do it all again he would do it the same way.

The window was open. In the parking lot, doors were being slammed and engines turned on. I listened to the cars until their noise was swallowed up in the roar of the traffic. Then children came to play and yell in the emptied parking lot. Sometimes a word came through quite clearly: a name, an insult, a call.

The judge stood up and said goodbye. He told me I could come again if I had any other questions, or if I wanted advice on my studies. And he would like to know our seminar group's evaluation and analysis of the trial.

I walked through the empty parking lot. One of the bigger boys told me how I could walk to the railroad station. Our car pool had driven back right after the session, and I had to take the train. It was a slow rush-hour train that stopped at every station; people got on and off. I sat at the window, surrounded by ever-changing passengers, conversations, smells. Outside, houses passed by, and roads, cars, trees, distant mountains, castles, and quarries. I took it all in and felt nothing. I was no longer upset at having been left, deceived, and used by Hanna. I no longer had to meddle with her. I felt the numbness with which I had followed the horrors of the trial settling over the emotions and thoughts of the past few weeks. It would be too much to say I was happy about this. But I felt it was right. It allowed me to return to and continue to live my everyday life.

CHAPTER SEVENTEEN

HE VERDICT was handed down at the end of June. Hanna was sentenced to life. The others received terms in jail.

The courtroom was as full as it had been at the beginning of the trial. People from the justice system, students from my university and the local one, a class of schoolchildren, domestic and foreign journalists, and the people who always find their way into courtrooms. It was loud. At first, no one noticed when the defendants were brought in. But then the spectators fell silent. The first to stop talking were those sitting up front near the defendants. They nudged their neighbors and turned around to those sitting behind them. "Look," they whispered, and those who looked fell silent too and nudged their neighbors and turned to those sitting behind them and whispered,

"Look!" Until eventually the whole courtroom was silent.

I don't know if Hanna knew how she looked, or maybe she wanted to look like that. She was wearing a black suit and a white blouse, and the cut of the suit and the tie that went with the blouse made her look as if she were in uniform. I have never seen the uniform of the women who worked for the SS. But I believed, and the spectators all believed, that before us we were seeing that uniform, and the woman who had worked for the SS in it, and all the crimes Hanna was accused of doing.

The spectators began to whisper again. Many were audibly outraged. They felt that Hanna was ridiculing the trial, the verdict, and themselves, they who had come to hear the verdict read out. They became more vociferous, and some of them began calling out what they thought of Hanna. But then the court entered the courtroom and after an irritated glance at Hanna, the judge announced the verdict. Hanna listened standing up, straight-backed, and absolutely motionless. She sat down during the reading of the reasons for the verdict. I did not take my eyes off her head and neck.

The entire verdict took several hours to read. When the trial was over and the defendants were being led away, I waited to see whether Hanna would look at me. I was sitting in the same place I always sat. But she looked straight ahead and through everything. A proud, wounded, lost, and infinitely tired look. A look that wished to see nothing and no one.

PART THREE

CHAPTER ONE

I SPENT THE summer after the trial in the
reading room of the university library. I arrived as the reading room opened and left when it
closed. On weekends I studied at home. I studied so
uninterruptedly, so obsessively, that the feelings and
thoughts that had been deadened by the trial remained deadened. I avoided contacts. I moved away
from home and rented a room. I brushed off the few
acquaintances who spoke to me in the reading room
or on my occasional visits to the movies.

The winter semester I was much the same way.
Nonetheless, I was asked if I would like to spend the
Christmas vacation with a group of students at a ski
lodge. Surprised, I accepted.

I wasn't a good skier, but I liked to ski and was
fast and kept up with the good ones. Sometimes

when I was on slopes that were beyond my ability, I risked falls and broken bones. I did this consciously. The other risk I was taking, and to which I succumbed, was one to which I was oblivious.

I was never cold. While the others skied in sweaters and jackets, I skied in a shirt. The others shook their heads and teased me about it, but I didn't take their worries seriously. I simply didn't feel cold. When I began to cough, I blamed it on the Austrian cigarettes. When I started to feel feverish, I enjoyed it. I felt weak and light at the same time, and all my senses were pleasingly muffled, cottony, padded. I floated.

Then I came down with a high fever and was taken to the hospital. By the time I left, the numbness was gone. All the questions and fears, accusations and self-accusations, all the horror and pain that had erupted during the trial and been immediately deadened were back, and back for good. I don't know what the doctors diagnose when someone isn't freezing even though he should be freezing. My own diagnosis is that the numbness had to overwhelm my body before it would let go of me, before I could let go of it.

When I had finished my studies and began my training, it was the summer of the student upheavals. I was interested in history and sociology, and while clerking with a judge I was still in the university often enough to know what was going on.

Knowing what was going on did not mean taking part—university and university reforms were no more interesting to me than the Vietcong and the Americans. As for the third and real theme of the student movement, coming to grips with the Nazi past, I felt so removed from the other students that I had no desire to agitate and demonstrate with them.

Sometimes I think that dealing with the Nazi past was not the reason for the generational conflict that drove the student movement, but merely the form it took. Parental expectations, from which every generation must free itself, were nullified by the fact that these parents had failed to measure up during the Third Reich, or after it ended. How could those who had committed Nazi crimes or watched them happen or looked away while they were happening or tolerated the criminals among them after 1945 or even accepted them—how could they have anything to say to their children? But on the other hand, the Nazi past was an issue even for children who couldn't accuse their parents of anything, or didn't want to. For them, coming to grips with the Nazi past was not merely the form taken by a generational conflict, it was the issue itself.

Whatever validity the concept of collective guilt may or may not have, morally and legally—for my generation of students it was a lived reality. It did not just apply to what had happened in the Third Reich. The fact that Jewish gravestones were being defaced with swastikas, that so many old Nazis had made careers in the courts, the administration, and the universities, that the Federal Republic did not recognize the State of Israel for many years, that emigration and resistance were handed down as traditions less often than a life of conformity—all this filled us with shame, even when we could point at the guilty parties. Pointing at the guilty parties did not free us from shame, but at least it overcame the suffering we went through on account of it. It converted the passive suffering of shame into energy, activity, aggression. And coming to grips with our parents' guilt took a great deal of energy.

I had no one to point at. Certainly not my parents, because I had nothing to accuse them of. The zeal for letting in the daylight, with which, as a member of the concentration camps seminar, I had condemned my father to shame, had passed, and it embarrassed me. But what other people in my social environment had done, and their guilt, were in any case a lot less bad than what Hanna had done. I had to point at Hanna. But the finger I pointed at her turned back to me. I had loved her. Not only had I loved her, I had chosen her. I tried to tell myself that I had known nothing of what she had done when I chose her. I tried to talk myself into the state of innocence in which children love their parents. But love of our parents is the only love for which we are not responsible.

And perhaps we are responsible even for the love we feel for our parents. I envied other students back then who had dissociated themselves from their parents and thus from the entire generation of perpetrators, voyeurs, and the willfully blind, accommodators and accepters, thereby overcoming perhaps not their shame, but at least their suffering because of the shame. But what gave rise to the swaggering self-righteousness I so often encountered among these students? How could one feel guilt and shame, and at the same time parade one's self-righteousness? Was their dissociation of themselves from their parents mere rhetoric: sounds and noise that were supposed to drown out the fact that their love for their parents made them irrevocably complicit in their crimes?

These thoughts did not come until later, and even later they brought no comfort. How could it be a comfort that the pain I went through because of my love for Hanna was, in a way, the fate of my generation, a German fate, and that it was only more difficult for me to evade, more difficult for me to manage than for others. All the same, it would have been good for me back then to be able to feel I was part of my generation.

CHAPTER TWO

I MARRIED WHILE I was still clerking. Gertrud and I had met at the ski lodge, and when the others left at the end of vacation, she stayed behind until I was released from the hospital and she could take me home. She was also studying law; we studied together, passed our exams together, and began our clerking together. We got married when Gertrud got pregnant.

I did not tell her about Hanna. Who, I thought, wants to know about the other's earlier relationships, if he or she is not the fulfillment of their promise? Gertrud was smart, efficient, and loyal, and if our life had involved running a farm with lots of farmhands and maids, lots of children, lots of work, and no time for each other, it would have been fulfilling and happy. But our life was a three-room apartment in a modern building on the edge of the city, our daughter Julia and Gertrud's and my work as legal clerks. I could never stop comparing the way it was with Gertrud and the way it had been with Hanna; again and again, Gertrud and I would hold each other, and I would feel that something was wrong, that she was wrong, that she moved wrong and felt wrong, smelled wrong and tasted wrong. I thought I would get over it. I hoped it would go away. I wanted to be free of Hanna. But I never got over the feeling that something was wrong.

We got divorced when Julia was five. Neither of us could keep things going; we parted without bitterness and retained our loyalty to each other. It tormented me that we were denying Julia the sense of warmth and safety she obviously craved. When Gertrud and I were open and warm with each other, Julia swam in it like a fish in water. She was in her element. When she sensed tension between us, she ran from one to the other to assure us that we were good and she loved us. She longed for a little brother and probably would have been happy with more siblings. For a long time, she didn't understand what divorce meant; when I came to visit, she wanted me to stay, and when she came to visit me, she wanted Gertrud to come too. When it was time to go, and she watched me from the window, and I had to get into the car under her sad gaze, it broke my heart. And I had the feeling that what we were denying her was not only her wish, but her right. We had cheated her of her rights by getting divorced, and the fact that we did it together didn't halve the guilt.

I tried to approach my later relationships better, and to get into them more deeply. I admitted to myself that a woman had to move and feel a bit like Hanna, smell and taste a bit like her for things to be good between us. I told them about Hanna. And I told them more about myself than I had told Gertrud; they had to be able to make sense of whatever they might find disconcerting in my behavior and moods. But the women didn't want to hear that much. I remember Helen, an American literary critic who stroked my back silently and soothingly as I talked, and continued to stroke me just as silently and soothingly after I'd stopped speaking. Gesina, a psychoanalyst, thought I needed to work through my relationship with my mother. Did it not strike me that my mother hardly appeared in my story at all? Hilke, a dentist, kept asking about the time before we met, but immediately forgot whatever I told her. So I stopped talking about it. There's no need to talk, because the truth of what one says lies in what one does.

CHAPTER THREE

*A*s i was taking my second state exam,
the professor who had given the concentration camps seminar died. Gertrud came across the
obituary in the newspaper. The funeral was at the
mountain cemetery. Did I want to go?

I didn't. The burial was on a Thursday afternoon,
and on both Thursday and Friday morning I had to
take written exams. Also, the professor and I had
never been particularly close. And I didn't like fu-
nerals. And I didn't want to be reminded of the trial.

But it was already too late. The memory had been
awakened, and when I came out of the exam on
Thursday, it was as if I had an appointment with the
past that I couldn't miss. I did something I never did
otherwise: I took the streetcar. This in itself was an
encounter with the past, like returning to a place

that once was familiar but has changed its appearance. When Hanna worked for the streetcar company, there were long streetcars made up of two or three carriages, platforms at the front and back, running boards along the platforms that you could jump onto when the streetcar had pulled away from the stop, and a cord running through the cars that the conductor rang to signal departure. In summer there were streetcars with open platforms. The conductor sold, punched, and inspected tickets, called out the stations, signaled departures, kept an eye on the children who pushed their way onto the platforms, fought with passengers who jumped off and on, and denied further entry if the car was full. There were cheerful, witty, serious, grouchy, and coarse conductors, and the temperament or mood of the conductor often defined the atmosphere in the car. How stupid of me that after the failed surprise on the ride to Schwetzingen, I had been afraid to waylay Hanna and see what she was like as a conductor.

I got onto the conductor-less streetcar and rode to the mountain cemetery. It was a cold autumn day with a cloudless, hazy sky and a yellow sun that no longer gave off any heat, the kind you can look at directly without hurting your eyes. I had to search awhile before finding the grave where the funeral ceremony was being held. I walked beneath tall, bare trees, between old gravestones. Occasionally I met a cemetery gardener or an old woman with a watering can and gardening shears. It was absolutely still, and from a distance I could hear the hymn being sung at the professor's grave.

I stopped a little way off and studied the small group of mourners. Some of them were clearly eccentrics and misfits. In the eulogies for the professor, there were hints that he himself had withdrawn from the pressures of society and thus lost contact with it, remaining a loner and thereby becoming something of an oddball himself.

I recognized a former member of the concentration camps seminar. He had taken his exams before me, had become a practicing attorney, and then opened a pub; he was dressed in a long red coat. He came to speak to me when everything was over and I was making my way to the cemetery gate. "We were in the same seminar—don't you remember?"

"I do." We shook hands.

"I was always at the trial on Wednesdays, and sometimes I gave you a lift." He laughed. "You were there every day, every day and every week. Can you say why, now?" He looked at me, good-natured and ready to pounce, and I remembered that I had noticed this look even in the seminar.

"I was very interested in the trial."

"You were very interested in the trial?" He laughed again. "The trial, or the defendant you were always staring at? The only one who was reasonably good-looking. We all used to wonder what was going on between you and her, but none of us dared ask. We were so terribly sensitive and considerate back then. Do you remember . . ." He recalled another member of the seminar, who stuttered or lisped and held forth incessantly, most of it nonsense, and to whom we listened as though his words were gold. He went on to talk about other members of the seminar, what they were like back then and what they were doing now. He talked and talked. But I knew he would get back to me eventually and ask: "So—what was going on between you and the defendant?" And I didn't know what to answer, how to betray, confess, parry.

Then we were at the entrance to the cemetery, and he asked. A streetcar was just pulling away from the stop and I called out, "Bye," and ran off as though I could jump onto the running board, ran alongside the streetcar beating the flat of my hand against the door, and something happened that I wouldn't have believed possible, hadn't even hoped for. The streetcar stopped, the door opened, and I got on.

*A*FTER MY state exam, I had to decide on a profession within the law. I gave myself a little time; Gertrud, who immediately began working in the judiciary, had her hands full, and we were happy that I could remain at home and take care of Julia. Once Gertrud had got over all the difficulties of getting started and Julia was in kindergarten, I had to make a decision.

I had a hard time of it. I didn't see myself in any of the roles I had seen lawyers play at Hanna's trial. Prosecution seemed to me as grotesque a simplification as defense, and judging was the most grotesque oversimplification of all. Nor could I see myself as an administrative official; I had worked at a local government office during my training, and found its rooms, corridors, smells, and employees gray, sterile, and dreary.

That did not leave many legal careers, and I don't know what I would have done if a professor of legal history had not offered me a research job. Gertrud said it was an evasion, an escape from the challenges and responsibilities of life, and she was right. I escaped and was relieved that I could do so. After all, it wasn't forever, I told both her and myself; I was young enough to enter any solid branch of the legal profession after a few years of legal history. But it was forever; the first escape was followed by a second, when I moved from the university to a research institution, seeking and finding a niche in which I could pursue my interest in legal history, in which I needed no one and disturbed no one.

Now escape involves not just running away, but arriving somewhere. And the past I arrived in as a legal historian was no less alive than the present. It is also not true, as outsiders might assume, that one can merely observe the richness of life in the past, whereas one can participate in the present. Doing history means building bridges between the past and the present, observing both banks of the river, taking an active part on both sides. One of my areas of research was law in the Third Reich, and here it is particularly obvious how the past and present come together in a single reality. Here, escape is not a preoccupation with the past, but a determined focus on the present and the future that is blind to the legacy of the past which brands us and with which we must live.

In saying this, I do not mean to conceal how gratifying it was to plunge into different stretches of the past that were not so urgently connected to the present. I felt it for the first time when I was working on the legal codes and drafts of the Enlightenment. They were based on the belief that a good order is intrinsic to the world, and that therefore the world can be brought into good order. To see how legal provisions were created paragraph by paragraph out of this belief as solemn guardians of this good order, and worked into laws that strove for beauty and by their very beauty for truth, made me happy. For a long time I believed that there was progress in the history of law, a development towards greater beauty and truth, rationality and humanity, despite terrible setbacks and retreats. Once it became clear to me that this belief was a chimera, I began playing with a different image of the course of legal history. In this one it still has a purpose, but the goal it finally attains, after countless disruptions, confusions, and delusions, is the beginning, its own original starting point, which once reached must be set off from again.

I reread the *Odyssey* at that time, which I had first read in school and remembered as the story of a homecoming. But it is not the story of a homecoming. How could the Greeks, who knew that one never enters the same river twice, believe in home-coming? Odysseus does not return home to stay, but to set off again. The *Odyssey* is the story of motion both purposeful and purposeless, successful and futile. What else is the history of law?

CHAPTER FIVE

IT BEGAN WITH the *Odyssey*. I read it after Gertrud and I had separated. There were many nights when I couldn't sleep for more than a few hours; I would lie awake, and when I switched on the light and picked up a book, my eyes closed, and when I put the book down and turned off the light, I was wide awake again. So I read aloud, and my eyes didn't close. And because in all my confused half-waking thoughts that swirled in tormenting circles of memories and dreams around my marriage and my daughter and my life, it was always Hanna who predominated, I read to Hanna. I read to Hanna on tape.

It was several months before I sent off the tapes. At first I didn't want to send just bits of it, so I waited until I had recorded all of the *Odyssey*. Then I began to wonder if Hanna would find the *Odyssey* sufficiently interesting, so I recorded what I read next after the *Odyssey,* stories by Schnitzler and Chekhov. Then I put off calling the court that had convicted Hanna to find out where she was serving her sentence. Finally I had everything together, Hanna's address in a prison near the city where she had been tried and convicted, a cassette player, and the cassettes, numbered from Chekhov to Schnitzler to Homer. And so finally I sent off the package with the machine and the tapes.

Recently I found the notebook in which I entered what I recorded for Hanna over the years. The first twelve titles were obviously all entered at the same time; at first I probably just read, and then realized that if I didn't keep notes I would not remember what I had already recorded. Next to the subsequent titles there is sometimes a date, sometimes none, but even without dates I know that I sent Hanna the first package in the eighth year of her imprisonment, and the last in the eighteenth. In the eighteenth, her plea for clemency was granted.

In general I read to Hanna the things I wanted to read myself at any given moment. With the *Odyssey,* I found at first that it was hard to take in as much when I read aloud as when I read silently to myself. But that changed. The disadvantage of reading aloud remained the fact that it took longer. But books read aloud also stayed long in my memory.

Even today, I can remember things in them absolutely clearly.

But I also read books I already knew and loved. So Hanna got to hear a great deal of Keller and Fontane, Heine and Mörike. For a long time I didn't dare to read poetry, but eventually I really enjoyed it, and I learned many of the poems I read by heart. I can still say them today.

Taken together, the titles in the notebook testify to a great and fundamental confidence in bourgeois culture. I do not ever remember asking myself whether I should go beyond Kafka, Frisch, Johnson, Bachmann, and Lenz, and read experimental literature, literature in which I did not recognize the story or like any of the characters. To me it was obvious that experimental literature was experimenting with the reader, and Hanna didn't need that and neither did I.

When I began writing myself, I read these pieces aloud to her as well. I waited until I had dictated my handwritten text, and revised the typewritten version, and had the feeling that now it was finished. When I read it aloud, I could tell if the feeling was right or not. And if not, I could revise it and record a new version over the old. But I didn't like doing that. I wanted to have my reading be the culmination. Hanna became the court before which once again I concentrated all my energies, all my creativity, all my critical imagination. After that, I could send the manuscript to the publisher.

I never made a personal remark on the tapes, never asked after Hanna, never told her anything about myself. I read out the title, the name of the author, and the text. When the text was finished, I waited a moment, closed the book, and pressed the Stop button.

*I*N THE FOURTH year of our word-driven, wordless contact, a note arrived. "Kid, the last story was especially nice. Thank you. Hanna."

It was lined paper, torn out of a notebook, and cut smooth. The message was right up at the top, and filled three lines. It was written in blue smudged ballpoint pen. Hanna had been pressing hard on the pen; the letters went through to the other side. She had also written the address with a great deal of pressure; the imprint was legible on the bottom and top halves of the paper, which was folded in the middle.

At first glance, one might have taken it for a child's handwriting. But what is clumsy and awkward in children's handwriting was forceful here.

You could see the resistance Hanna had had to overcome to make the lines into letters and the letters
into words. A child's hand will wander off this way
and that, and has to be kept on track. Hanna's hand
didn't want to go anywhere and had to be forced.
The lines that formed the letters started again each
time on the upstroke, the downstroke, and before
the curves and loops. And each letter was a victory
over a fresh struggle, and had a new slant or slope,
and often the wrong height or width.

I read the note and was filled with joy and jubila-
tion. "She can write, she can write!" In these years I
had read everything I could lay my hands on to do
with illiteracy. I knew about the helplessness in
everyday activities, finding one's way or finding an
address or choosing a meal in a restaurant, about
how illiterates anxiously stick to prescribed patterns
and familiar routines, about how much energy it
takes to conceal one's inability to read and write, energy lost to actual living. Illiteracy is dependence. By
finding the courage to learn to read and write,
Hanna had advanced from dependence to independence, a step towards liberation.

Then I looked at Hanna's handwriting and saw
how much energy and struggle the writing had cost
her. I was proud of her. At the same time, I was sorry
for her, sorry for her delayed and failed life, sorry for
the delays and failures of life in general. I thought
that if the right time gets missed, if one has refused

or been refused something for too long, it's too late, even if it is finally tackled with energy and received with joy. Or is there no such thing as "too late"? Is there only "late," and is "late" always better than "never"? I don't know.

After the first note came a steady stream of others. They were always only a few lines, a thank you, a wish to hear more of a particular author or to hear no more, a comment on an author or a poem or a story or a character in a novel, an observation about prison. "The forsythia is already in flower in the yard" or "I like the fact that there have been so many storms this summer" or "From my window I can see the birds flocking to fly south"—often it was Hanna's note that first made me pay attention to the forsythia, the summer storms, or the flocks of birds. Her remarks about literature often landed astonishingly on the mark. "Schnitzler barks, Stefan Zweig is a dead dog" or "Keller needs a woman" or "Goethe's poems are like tiny paintings in beautiful frames" or "Lenz must write on a typewriter." Because she knew nothing about the authors, she assumed they were contemporaries, unless something indicated this was obviously impossible. I was astonished at how much older literature can actually be read as if it were contemporary; to anyone ignorant of history, it would be easy to see ways of life in earlier times simply as ways of life in foreign countries.

I never wrote to Hanna. But I kept reading to her. When I spent a year in America, I sent cassettes from there. When I was on vacation or was particularly busy, it might take longer for me to finish the next cassette; I never established a definite rhythm, but sent cassettes sometimes every week or two weeks, and sometimes only every three or four weeks. I didn't worry that Hanna might not need my cassettes now that she had learned to read by herself. She could read as well. Reading aloud was my way of speaking to her, with her.

I kept all her notes. The handwriting changed. At first she forced the letters into the same slant and the right height and width. Once she had managed that, she became lighter and more confident. Her handwriting never became fluid, but it acquired something of the severe beauty that characterizes the writing of old people who have written little in their lives.

CHAPTER SEVEN

At the time I never thought about the fact that Hanna would be released one day. The exchange of notes and cassettes was so normal and familiar, and Hanna was both close and removed in such an easy way, that I could have continued the situation indefinitely. That was comfortable and selfish, I know.

Then came the letter from the prison warden.

For years you and Frau Schmitz have corresponded with each other. This is the only contact Frau Schmitz has with the outside world, and so I am turning to you, although I do not know how close your relationship is, and whether you are a relative or a friend.

Next year Frau Schmitz will again make an appeal for clemency, and I expect the parole board to grant the appeal.

She will then be released quite shortly—after eighteen years in prison. Of course we can find or try to find her an apartment and a job; a job will be difficult at her age, even though she is in excellent health and has shown great skill in our sewing shop. But rather than us taking care of her, it would be better for relatives or friends to do so, to have the released prisoner live nearby, and keep her company and give her support. You cannot imagine how lonely and help-less one can be on the outside after eighteen years in prison.

Frau Schmitz can take care of herself quite well, and manages on her own. It would be enough if you could find her a small apartment and a job, visit her, and invite her to your house occasionally during the first weeks and months and make sure she knows about the programs offered by the local congregation, adult education, family support groups, and so on.

It is not easy, after eighteen years, to go into the city for the first time, go shopping, deal with the authorities, go to a restaurant. Doing it with someone else helps.

I have noticed that you do not visit Frau Schmitz. If you did, I would not have written to you, but would have asked to talk to you during one of your visits. Now it seems as if you will have to visit her before she is released. Please come and see me at that opportunity.

The letter closed with sincere greetings which I did not think referred to me, but to the fact that the warden was sincere about the issue. I had heard of her; her institution was considered extraordinary, and her opinion on questions of penal reform carried weight. I liked her letter.

But I did not like what was coming my way. Of course I would have to see about a job and an apartment, and I did. Friends who neither used nor rented out the apartment attached to their house agreed to let it to Hanna at a low rent. The Greek tailor who occasionally altered my clothes was willing to employ Hanna; his sister, who ran the tailoring business with him, wanted to return to Greece. And long before Hanna could have used them, I looked into the social services and educational programs run by churches and secular organizations. But I put off the visit to Hanna.

Precisely because she was both close and removed in such an easy way, I didn't want to visit her. I had the feeling she could only be what she was to me at an actual distance. I was afraid that the small, light, safe world of notes and cassettes was too artificial and too vulnerable to withstand actual closeness. How could we meet face to face without everything that had happened between us coming to the surface?

So the year passed without me going to the prison. For a long time I heard nothing from the warden; a letter in which I described the housing and job situation for Hanna went unanswered. She was probably expecting to talk to me when I visited Hanna. She had no way to know that I was not only putting off this visit, but avoiding it. Finally, however, the decision came down to pardon and release Hanna, and the warden called me. Could I come now? Hanna was getting out in a week.

CHAPTER EIGHT

I WENT THE next Sunday. It was my first visit to a prison. I was searched at the entrance, and a number of doors were unlocked and locked along the way. But the building was new and bright, and in the inner area the doors were open, allowing the women to move about freely. At the end of a corridor a door opened to the outside, onto a little lawn with lots of people and trees and benches. I looked around, searching. The guard who had brought me pointed to a nearby bench in the shade of a chestnut tree.

Hanna? The woman on the bench was Hanna? Gray hair, a face with deep furrows on brow and cheeks and around the mouth, and a heavy body. She was wearing a light blue dress that was too tight and stretched across her breasts, stomach, and thighs.

Her hands lay in her lap holding a book. She wasn't reading it. Over the top of her half-glasses, she was watching a woman throwing bread crumbs to a couple of sparrows. Then she realized that she was being watched, and turned her face to me.

I saw the expectation in her face, saw it light up with joy when she recognized me, watched her eyes scan my face as I approached, saw them seek, inquire, then look uncertain and hurt, and saw the light go out of her face. When I reached her, she smiled a friendly, weary smile. "You've grown up, kid." I sat down beside her and she took my hand.

In the past, I had particularly loved her smell. She always smelled fresh, freshly washed or of fresh laundry or fresh sweat or freshly loved. Sometimes she used perfume, I don't know which one, and its smell, too, was more fresh than anything else. Under these fresh smells was another, heavy, dark, sharp smell. Often I would sniff at her like a curious animal, starting with her throat and shoulders, which smelled freshly washed, soaking up the fresh smell of sweat between her breasts mixed in her armpits with the other smell, then finding this heavy dark smell almost pure around her waist and stomach and between her legs with a fruity tinge that excited me; I would also sniff at her legs and feet—her thighs, where the heavy smell disappeared, the hollows of her knees again with that light, fresh smell of sweat, and her feet, which smelled of soap or leather or tiredness. Her back and arms had no special smell; they smelled of nothing and yet they smelled of her, and the palms of her hands smelled of the day and of work—the ink of the tickets, the metal of the ticket puncher, onions or fish or frying fat, soapsuds or the heat of the iron. When they are freshly washed, hands betray none of this. But soap only covers the smells, and after a time they return, faint, blending into a single scent of the day and work, a scent of work and day's end, of evening, of coming home and being at home.

I sat next to Hanna and smelled an old woman. I don't know what makes up this smell, which I recognize from grandmothers and elderly aunts, and which hangs in the rooms and halls of old-age homes like a curse. Hanna was too young for it.

I moved closer. I had seen that I had disappointed her before, and I wanted to do better, make up for it.

"I'm glad you're getting out."

"You are?"

"Yes, and I'm glad you'll be nearby." I told her about the apartment and the job I had found for her, about the cultural and social programs available in that part of the city, about the public library. "Do you read a lot?"

"A little. Being read to is nicer." She looked at me. "That's over now, isn't it?"

"Why should it be over?" But I couldn't see myself talking into cassettes for her or meeting her to read aloud. "I was so glad and so proud of you when you learned to read. And what nice letters you wrote me!" That was true; I had admired her and been glad, because she was reading and she wrote to me. But I could feel how little my admiration and happiness were worth compared to what learning to read and write must have cost Hanna, how meager they must have been if they could not even get me to answer her, visit her, talk to her. I had granted Hanna a small niche, certainly an important niche, one from which I gained something and for which I did something, but not a place in my life.

But why should I have given her a place in my life? I reacted indignantly against my own bad conscience at the thought that I had reduced her to a niche. "Didn't you ever think about the things that were discussed at the trial, before the trial? I mean, didn't you ever think about them when we were together, when I was reading to you?"

"Does that bother you very much?" But she didn't wait for an answer. "I always had the feeling that no one understood me anyway, that no one knew who I was and what made me do this or that. And you know, when no one understands you, then no one can call you to account. Not even the court could call me to account. But the dead can. They understand. They don't even have to have been there, but if they were, they understand even better. Here in prison they were with me a lot. They came every night, whether

I wanted them or not. Before the trial I could still chase them away when they wanted to come."

She waited to see if I had anything to say, but I couldn't think of anything. At first, I wanted to say that I wasn't able to chase anything away. But it wasn't true. You can chase someone away by setting them in a niche.

"Are you married?"

"I was. Gertrud and I have been divorced for many years and our daughter is at boarding school; I hope she won't stay there for the last years of school, and will move in with me." Now I waited to see if she would say or ask anything. But she was silent. "I'll pick you up next week, all right?"

"All right."

"Quietly, or can there be a little noise and hoopla?"

"Quietly."

"Okay, I'll pick you up quietly, with no music or champagne."

I stood up, and she stood up. We looked at each other. The bell had rung twice, and the other women had already gone inside. Once again her eyes scanned my face. I took her in my arms, but she didn't feel right.

"Take care, kid."

"You too."

So we said goodbye, even before we had to separate inside.

CHAPTER NINE

*T*HE FOLLOWING week was particularly busy. I don't remember whether I was under actual pressure to finish the lecture I was working on, or only under self-inflicted pressure to work and succeed.

The idea I had had when I began working on the lecture was no good. When I began to revise it, where I expected to find meaning and consistency, I encountered one non sequitur after another. Instead of accepting this, I kept searching, harassed, obsessed, anxious, as though reality itself could fail along with my concept of it, and I was ready to twist or exaggerate or play down my own findings. I got into a state of strange disquiet; I could go to sleep if I went to bed late, but a few hours later I would be wide awake, until I decided to get up and continue reading or writing.

I also did what needed to be done to prepare for Hanna's release. I furnished her apartment with furniture from IKEA and some old pieces, advised the Greek tailor that Hanna would be coming in, and brought my information about social services and educational programs up to date. I bought groceries, put books on the bookshelves, and hung pictures. I had a gardener come to tidy up the little garden surrounding the terrace outside the living room. I did all this with unnatural haste and doggedness; it was all too much for me.

But it was just enough to prevent me from thinking about my visit to Hanna. Only occasionally, when I was driving my car, or when I was in Hanna's apartment, did thoughts of it get the upper hand and trigger memories. I saw her on the bench, her eyes fixed on me, saw her at the swimming pool, her face turned to me, and again had the feeling that I had betrayed her and owed her something. And again I rebelled against this feeling; I accused her, and found it both shabby and too easy, the way she had wriggled out of her guilt. Allowing no one but the dead to demand an accounting, reducing guilt and atonement to insomnia and bad feelings—where did that leave the living? But what I meant was not the living, it was me. Did I not have my own accounting to demand of her? What about me?

On the afternoon before I was due to pick her up, I called the prison. First I spoke to the warden.

"I'm a bit nervous. You know, normally people aren't released after such long sentences before spending a few hours or days outside. Frau Schmitz refused this. It won't be easy for her."

Then I spoke to Hanna.

"Think about what we should do tomorrow. Whether you want to go straight home, or whether we might go to the woods or the river."

"I'll think about it. You're still a big planner, aren't you?"

That annoyed me. It annoyed me the way it did when girlfriends told me I wasn't spontaneous enough, that I operated too much through my head and not enough through my heart.

She could tell by my silence that I was annoyed, and laughed. "Don't be cross, kid. I didn't mean anything by it."

I had met Hanna again on the benches as an old woman. She had looked like an old woman and smelled like an old woman. I hadn't noticed her voice at all. Her voice had stayed young.

CHAPTER TEN

NEXT MORNING, Hanna was dead. She had hanged herself at daybreak.

When I arrived, I was taken to the warden. I saw her for the first time—a small, thin woman with dark blond hair and glasses. She seemed insignificant until she began to speak, with force and warmth and a severe gaze and energetic use of both hands and arms. She asked me about my telephone conversation of the night before and the meeting the previous week. Had I picked up any signals, had it made me fear for her? I said no. Indeed, I had had no suspicions or fears that I had ignored.

"How did you get to know each other?"

"We lived in the same neighborhood."

She looked at me searchingly, and I saw that I would have to say more.

"We lived in the same neighborhood and we got to know each other and became friends. When I was a young student, I was at the trial that convicted her."

"Why did you send Frau Schmitz cassettes?"

I was silent.

"You knew that she was illiterate, didn't you? How did you know?"

I shrugged my shoulders. I didn't see what business the story of Hanna and me was of hers. Tears were filling my chest and throat, and I was afraid I wouldn't be able to speak. I didn't want to cry in front of her.

She must have seen how I was feeling. "Come with me, I'll show you Frau Schmitz's cell." She went ahead, but kept turning around to tell me things or explain them to me. Here is where there had been a terrorist attack, here was the sewing shop where Hanna had worked, this is where Hanna once held a sit-down strike until cuts in library funding were reinstated, this was the way to the library. She stopped in front of the cell. "Frau Schmitz didn't pack. You'll see her cell the way she lived in it."

Bed, closet, table, chair, a shelf on the wall over the table, a sink and toilet in the corner behind the door. Glass bricks instead of window glass. The table was bare. The shelf held books, an alarm clock, a stuffed bear, two mugs, instant coffee, tea tins, the cassette machine, and on two lower shelves, the cassettes I had made.

"They aren't all here."

The warden had followed my glance. "Frau Schmitz always lent some tapes to the aid society for blind prisoners."

I went over to the bookshelf. Primo Levi, Elie Wiesel, Tadeusz Borowski, Jean Améry—the literature of the victims, next to the autobiography of Rudolf Hess, Hannah Arendt's report on Eichmann in Jerusalem, and scholarly literature on the camps.

"Did Hanna read these?"

"Well, at least she ordered them with care. Several years ago I had to get her a general concentration-camp bibliography, and then one or two years ago she asked me to suggest some books on women in the camps, both prisoners and guards; I wrote to the Institute for Contemporary History, and they sent a specialized bibliography. As soon as Frau Schmitz learned to read, she began to read about the concentration camps."

Above the bed hung many small pictures and slips of paper. I knelt on the bed and read. There were quotations, poems, little articles, even recipes that Hanna had written down or cut out like pictures from newspapers and magazines. "Spring lets its blue banner flutter through the air again," "Cloud shadows fly across the fields"—the poems were all full of delight in nature, and yearning for it, and the pictures showed woods bright with spring, meadows spangled with flowers, autumn foliage and single

trees, a pasture by a stream, a cherry tree with ripe
red cherries, an autumnal chestnut flamed in yellow
and orange. A newspaper photograph showed an
older man and a younger man, both in dark suits,
shaking hands. In the young one, bowing to the
older one, I recognized myself. I was graduating
from school, and was getting a prize from the principal at the ceremony. That was a long time after
Hanna had left the city. Had Hanna, who could not
read, subscribed to the local paper in which my
photo appeared? In any case she must have gone to
some trouble to find out about the photo and get a
copy. And had she had it with her during the trial? I
felt the tears again in my chest and throat.

"She learned to read with you. She borrowed the
books you read on tape out of the library, and followed what she heard, word by word and sentence
by sentence. The tape machine couldn't handle all
that constant switching on and off, and rewinding
and fast-forwarding. It kept breaking down and
having to be repaired, and because that required per-
mission, I finally found out what Frau Schmitz was
doing. She didn't want to tell me at first; when she
also began to write, and asked me for a writing man-
ual, she didn't try to hide it any longer. She was also
just proud that she had succeeded, and wanted to
share her happiness."

As she spoke, I had continued to kneel, my eyes
on the pictures and notes, fighting back tears. When

I turned around and sat down on the bed, she said, "She so hoped you would write. You were the only one she got mail from, and when the mail was distributed and she said 'No letter for me?' she wasn't talking about the packages the tapes came in. Why did you never write?"

I still said nothing. I could not have spoken; all I could have done was to stammer and weep.

She went to the shelf, picked up a tea tin, sat down next to me, and took a folded sheet of paper from her suit pocket. "She left a letter for me, a sort of will. I'll read the part that concerns you." She unfolded the sheet of paper. "There is still money in the lavender tea tin. Give it to Michael Berg; he should send it, along with the 7,000 marks in the bank, to the daughter who survived the fire in the church with her mother. She should decide what to do with it. And tell him I say hello to him."

So she had not left any message for me. Did she intend to hurt me? Or punish me? Or was her soul so tired that she could only do and write what was absolutely necessary? "What was she like all those years?" I waited until I could go on. "And how was she these last few days?"

"For years and years she lived here the way you would live in a convent. As if she had moved here of her own accord and voluntarily subjected herself to our system, as if the rather monotonous work was a sort of meditation. She was greatly respected by the

other women, to whom she was friendly but re-
served. More than that, she had authority, she was
asked for her advice when there were problems, and
if she intervened in an argument, her decision was
accepted. Then a few years ago she gave up. She had
always taken care of herself personally, she was slen-
der despite her strong build, and meticulously clean.
But now she began to eat a lot and seldom washed;
she got fat and smelled. She didn't seem unhappy or
dissatisfied. In fact it was as though the retreat to the
convent was no longer enough, as though life in the
convent was still too sociable and talkative, and she
had to retreat even further, into a lonely cell safe
from all eyes, where looks, clothing, and smell
meant nothing. No, it would be wrong to say that
she had given up. She redefined her place in a way
that was right for her, but no longer impressed the
other women."

"And the last days?"

"She was the way she always was."

"Can I see her?"

She nodded, but remained seated. "Can the world
become so unbearable to someone after years of lone-
liness? Is it better to kill yourself than to return to
the world from the convent, from the hermitage?"
She turned to me. "Frau Schmitz didn't write anything about why she was going to kill herself. And
you won't say what there was between you that
might have led to Frau Schmitz's killing herself at

the end of the night before you were due to pick her up." She folded the piece of paper, put it away, stood up, and smoothed her skirt. "Her death is a blow to me, you see, and at the moment I'm very angry, at Frau Schmitz, and at you. But let's go."

She led the way again, this time silently. Hanna lay in the infirmary in a small cubicle. We could just fit between the wall and the stretcher. The warden pulled back the sheet.

A cloth had been tied around Hanna's head to hold up her chin until the onset of rigor mortis. Her face was neither particularly peaceful nor particularly agonized. It looked rigid and dead. As I looked and looked, the living face became visible in the dead, the young in the old. This is what must happen to old married couples, I thought: the young man is preserved in the old one for her, the beauty and grace of the young woman stay fresh in the old one for him. Why had I not seen this reflection a week ago?

I must not cry. After a time, when the warden looked at me questioningly, I nodded, and she spread the sheet over Hanna's face again.

CHAPTER ELEVEN

I T W A S A U T U M N before I could carry out Hanna's instructions. The daughter lived in New York, and I used a meeting in Boston as the occasion to bring her the money: a bank check plus the tea tin with the cash. I had written to her, introduced myself as a legal historian, and mentioned the trial. I told her I would be grateful for a chance to talk to her. She invited me to tea.

I took the train from Boston to New York. The woods were a triumphal parade of brown, yellow, orange, tawny red, and chestnut, and the flaming glowing scarlet of the maples. It made me think of the autumn pictures in Hanna's cell. When the rhythm of the wheels and the rocking of the car tired me, I dreamed of Hanna and myself in a house in the autumn-blazed hills that were lining our route.

Hanna was older than when I had met her and younger than when I had met her again, older than me, more attractive than in earlier years, more relaxed in her movements with age, more at home in her own body. I saw her getting out of the car and picking up shopping bags, saw her going through the garden into the house, saw her set down the bags and go upstairs ahead of me. My longing for Hanna became so strong that it hurt. I struggled against the longing, argued that it went against Hanna's and my reality, the reality of our ages, the reality of our circumstances. How could Hanna, who spoke no English, live in America? And she couldn't drive a car either.

I woke up and knew that Hanna was dead. I also knew that my desire had fixed on her without her being its object. It was the desire to come home.

The daughter lived in New York on a street near Central Park. The street was lined on both sides with old row houses of dark sandstone, with stoops of the same sandstone leading up to the front door on the first floor. This created an effect of severity—house after house with almost identical façades, stoop after stoop, trees only recently planted at regular intervals along the sidewalk, with a few yellowing leaves on thin twigs.

The daughter served tea by large windows looking out on the vest-pocket backyard gardens, some green and colorful and some merely collections of trash. As soon as we had sat down, the tea had been poured, and the sugar added and stirred, she switched from the English in which she had welcomed me, to German. "What brings you here?" The question was neither friendly nor unfriendly; her tone was absolutely matter-of-fact. Everything about her was matter-of-fact: her manner, her gestures, her dress. Her face was oddly ageless, the way faces look after being lifted. But perhaps it had set because of her early sufferings; I tried and failed to remember her face as it had been during the trial.

I told her about Hanna's death and her last wishes.

"Why me?"

"I suppose because you are the only survivor."

"And how am I supposed to deal with it?"

"However you think fit."

"And grant Frau Schmitz her absolution?"

At first I wanted to protest, but Hanna was indeed asking a great deal. Her years of imprisonment were not merely to be the required atonement: Hanna wanted to give them her own meaning, and she wanted this giving of meaning to be recognized. I said as much.

She shook her head. I didn't know if this meant she was refusing to accept my interpretation or refusing to grant Hanna the recognition.

"Could you not recognize it without granting her absolution?"

She laughed. "You like her, don't you? What was your relationship?"

I hesitated a moment. "I read aloud to her. It started when I was fifteen and continued while she was in prison."

"How did you . . ."

"I sent her tapes. Frau Schmitz was illiterate almost all her life; she only learned to read and write in prison."

"Why did you do all this?"

"When I was fifteen, we had a relationship."

"You mean you slept together?"

"Yes."

"That woman was truly brutal . . . did you ever get over the fact that you were only fifteen when she . . . No, you said yourself that you began reading to her again when she was in prison. Did you ever get married?"

I nodded.

"And the marriage was short and unhappy, and you never married again, and the child, if there is one, is in boarding school."

"That's true of thousands of people, it doesn't take a Frau Schmitz."

"Did you ever feel, when you had contact with her in those last years, that she knew what she had done to you?"

I shrugged my shoulders. "In any case, she knew what she had done to people in the camp and on the march. She didn't just tell me that, she dealt with it intensively during her last years in prison." I told her what the warden had said.

She stood up and took long strides up and down the room. "How much money is it?"

I went to the coat closet, where I had left my bag, and returned with the check and the tea tin. "Here."

She looked at the check and put it on the table. She opened the tin, emptied it, closed it again, and held it in her hand, her eyes riveted on it. "When I was a little girl, I had a tea tin for my treasures. Not like this, although these sorts of tea tins already existed, but one with Cyrillic letters, not one with a top you push in, but one you snap shut. I brought it with me to the camp, but then one day it was stolen from me."

"What was in it?"

"What you'd expect. A piece of hair from our poodle. Tickets to the operas my father took me to, a ring I won somewhere or found in a package—the tin wasn't stolen for what was in it. The tin itself, and what could be done with it, were worth a lot in the camp." She put the tin down on top of the check. "Do you have a suggestion for what to do with the money? Using it for something to do with the Holocaust would really seem like an absolution to me, and that is something I neither wish nor care to grant."

"For illiterates who want to learn to read and write. There must be nonprofit organizations, foundations, societies you could give the money to."

"I'm sure there are." She thought about it.

"Are there corresponding Jewish organizations?"

"You can depend on it, if there are organizations for something, then there are Jewish organizations for it. Illiteracy, it has to be admitted, is hardly a Jewish problem." She pushed the check and the money back to me. "Let's do it this way. You find out what kind of relevant Jewish organizations there are, here or in Germany, and you pay the money to the account of the organization that seems most plausible to you." She laughed. "If the recognition is so important, you can do it in the name of Hanna Schmitz." She picked up the tin again. "I'll keep the tin."

CHAPTER TWELVE

ALL THIS happened ten years ago. In the first few years after Hanna's death, I was tormented by the old questions of whether I had denied and betrayed her, whether I owed her something, whether I was guilty for having loved her. Sometimes I asked myself if I was responsible for her death. And sometimes I was in a rage at her and at what she had done to me. Until finally the rage faded and the questions ceased to matter. Whatever I had done or not done, whatever she had done or not to me—it was the path my life had taken.

Soon after her death, I decided to write the story of me and Hanna. Since then I've done it many times in my head, each time a little differently, each time with new images, and new strands of action and thought. Thus there are many different stories in addition to the one I have written. The guarantee that the written one is the right one lies in the fact that I wrote it and not the other versions. The written version wanted to be written, the many others did not.

At first I wanted to write our story in order to be free of it. But the memories wouldn't come back for that. Then I realized our story was slipping away from me and I wanted to recapture it by writing, but that didn't coax up the memories either. For the last few years I've left our story alone. I've made peace with it. And it came back, detail by detail and in such a fully rounded fashion, with its own direction and its own sense of completion, that it no longer makes me sad. What a sad story, I thought for so long. Not that I now think it was happy. But I think it is true, and thus the question of whether it is sad or happy has no meaning whatever.

At any rate, that's what I think when I just happen to think about it. But if something hurts me, the hurts I suffered back then come back to me, and when I feel guilty, the feelings of guilt return; if I yearn for something today, or feel homesick, I feel the yearnings and homesickness from back then. The tectonic layers of our lives rest so tightly one on top of the other that we always come up against earlier events in later ones, not as matter that has been fully formed and pushed aside, but absolutely present and alive. I understand this. Nevertheless, I sometimes find it hard to bear. Maybe I did write our story to be free of it, even if I never can be.

As soon as I returned from New York, I donated Hanna's money in her name to the Jewish League Against Illiteracy. I received a short, computer-generated letter in which the Jewish League thanked Ms. Hanna Schmitz for her donation. With the letter in my pocket, I drove to the cemetery, to Hanna's grave. It was the first and only time I stood there.